THE
HAUNTED
LIBRARY

Classic Ghost Stories

THE HAUNTED LIBRARY

Classic Ghost Stories

edited and introduced by
TANYA KIRK

First published 2016 by
The British Library
96 Euston Road
London NW1 2DB

Introductory material copyright © 2016 Tanya Kirk

Dates attributed to each story relate to first publication.

Cataloguing in Publication Data
A catalogue record for this book is available from the British Library

ISBN 978 0 7123 5604 6

Typeset by Tetragon, London
Printed in England by TJ International

CONTENTS

INTRODUCTION 7

Afterward (1910)
Edith Wharton 11

The Tractate Middoth (1911)
M.R. James 51

Bone to His Bone (1912)
E.G. Swain 75

The Whisperers (1912)
Algernon Blackwood 87

Fingers of a Hand (1920)
H.D. Everett 97

The Nature of the Evidence (1923)
May Sinclair 109

Mr. Tallent's Ghost (1926)
Mary Webb 125

The Lost Tragedy (1926)
Denis Mackail 143

The Book (1930)
Margaret Irwin 165

The Apple Tree (1931)
Elizabeth Bowen 187

Herodes Redivivus (1949)
A.N.L. Munby 205

The Work of Evil (1963)
William Croft Dickinson 223

INTRODUCTION

Anyone who has made an evening visit to the British Library's stacks, deep underground at the Euston Road building, can tell you that books have a sort of silent presence. During the day the basements are hives of activity as staff busily retrieve books and manuscripts and send them off to the reading rooms. But after retrieval ends and the library assistants go home, checking a reference down there can be eerily quiet, the only sound being the ghostly rattle of a London Underground train as it passes nearby. All those hundreds of years of people's voices, their lives and experiences, recorded in books that have passed through so many hands—the impressions they leave behind mean you never feel totally alone.

This feeling of the uncanny nature of books and libraries has proved rich subject matter for authors, particularly in the first half of the twentieth century—promoted perhaps in part by an interest in antiquarianism and the power of old tomes in an age of encroaching modernism and technology. On 28 October 1893, a fellow of King's College, Cambridge, known as Monty James, told a group of friends a couple of ghost stories he had written for their entertainment. The tales, 'Canon Alberic's Scrapbook' and 'Lost Hearts', established a new genre—the antiquarian ghost story, in which horrors are awoken by scholarly pursuits, and libraries and museums contain unknown terrors. Over 120 years later, James's particular brand of gothic fiction remains as effective as ever it was, and dozens of writers have found his typical settings a rich source of inspiration.

James wrote in a distinctive style—not gruesome, but rather full of masterful understatement, withholding information and giving a partial description of some horrific encounter in order to let the reader's own imagination conjure up the rest. He traced the history of the ghost story back to some of the earliest British gothic writers: Horace Walpole, whose novel *The Castle of Otranto* launched the gothic genre in 1764; Ann Radcliffe; and Matthew Lewis, although he felt that in all cases their ghosts were not entirely effective. He felt strongly that stories worked best when set in contemporary, ordinary settings, and some of his scariest scenes take place in banal locations such as on board a train. The iconic horror actor Christopher Lee observed: "He wrote his stories so that we might feel just as if we were reading a newspaper, and his characters seemed at first impression to be the kind you could meet on any street. Then by dint of one phrase or sentence a very different picture would emerge from such an apparently normal situation. To me, that is the very essence of terror." In the James story included in this book, 'The Tractate Middoth', a simple bit of confusion (about whether or not a particular book at Cambridge University Library is already in use by a reader) proves to be unexpectedly terrifying in just the way Lee describes.

These twelve stories all take up the theme of cursed or haunted books, manuscripts and libraries, made so popular by M.R. James's work. Some of the writers in this book, such as E.G. Swain, A.N.L. Munby and William Croft Dickinson, were very directly inspired by James—Swain was even a friend and contemporary of his at Cambridge; the other two, although later, were from similar scholarly backgrounds. Whereas James told his stories to friends around a cheerfully blazing fire on Christmas Eve, Munby wrote his to entertain his fellow POWs at a camp in Germany during the Second World War, varied evidence of the escapist pleasure we get from hearing a scary story.

A couple of the tales are comic in tone—Mary Webb's 'Mr. Tallent's Ghost' and Denis Mackail's 'The Lost Tragedy', both of which were published in Lady Cynthia Asquith's famous collection *The Ghost Book* in 1926. Others speak of contemporary interests in the supernatural—H.D. Everett's 'Fingers of a Hand', which deals with automatic writing, and May Sinclair's 'The Nature of the Evidence', which was inspired by Freud's theory of the subconscious and the Uncanny, and the nature of relationships in a new era of psychological awareness. Two stories ('The Book' by Margaret Irwin, and 'The Work of Evil' by William Croft Dickinson) deal with evil books, which control their readers and coerce them into devilishness. And in both Edith Wharton's 'Afterward', the earliest story printed here, and in Elizabeth Bowen's 'The Apple Tree', one of the most recent, the libraries of country houses are the scenes of unusual variants on the traditional haunted house narrative.

Writers are always haunted by the ghosts of books—both their own and those of others. Perhaps this is why the haunted library motif has proved such a tempting one. Speaking for myself, it is the story 'The Whisperers' by Algernon Blackwood which best evokes the eerie feeling I get in the library stacks, after dark. I hope some of you will know exactly what I mean.

TANYA KIRK

Lead Curator, Printed Heritage Collections 1601–1900
The British Library

AFTERWARD (1910)

Edith Wharton (1862–1937)

Born into a privileged New York family, but later unhappily married, Edith Wharton is today renowned for novels such as *The House of Mirth* (1905) and *Ethan Frome* (1911) dealing with society's repression of women and the resulting difficulties in having a successful relationship. Within her novels, Wharton was adept at incorporating gothic motifs to represent a sense of feeling trapped and out of control, but she also wrote ghost stories where these themes could be explored more explicitly.

In this story, first published in the *Century Magazine* in 1910, an American woman settles in a country house in Dorset with her investor husband. As was common in a period when women were not considered capable of understanding the world of finance, she knows and understands very little of his business. The house, complete with ornate historic library, is a representation of the old world of Europe that they are buying into by living there, and the story opens with them longing for a ghost to make the house truly authentic, a wish which becomes increasingly ironic.

"OH, THERE *IS* ONE, OF COURSE, BUT YOU'LL NEVER KNOW it."

The assertion, laughingly flung out six months earlier in a bright June garden, came back to Mary Boyne with a new perception of its significance as she stood, in the December dusk, waiting for the lamps to be brought into the library.

The words had been spoken by their friend Alida Stair, as they sat at tea on her lawn at Pangbourne, in reference to the very house of which the library in question was the central, the pivotal "feature". Mary Boyne and her husband, in quest of a country place in one of the southern or southwestern counties, had, on their arrival in England, carried their problem straight to Alida Stair, who had successfully solved it in her own case; but it was not until they had rejected, almost capriciously, several practical and judicious suggestions that she threw out: "Well, there's Lyng, in Dorsetshire. It belongs to Hugo's cousins, and you can get it for a song."

The reason she gave for its being obtainable on these terms—its remoteness from a station, its lack of electric light, hot-water pipes, and other vulgar necessities—were exactly those pleading in its favour with two romantic Americans perversely in search of the economic drawbacks which were associated, in their tradition, with unusual architectural felicities.

"I should never believe I was living in an old house unless I was thoroughly uncomfortable," Ned Boyne, the more extravagant of the two, had jocosely insisted; "the least hint of 'convenience' would make me think it had been bought out of an exhibition, with the pieces numbered, and set up again." And they had proceeded to enumerate, with humorous precision, their various doubts and demands, refusing to believe that the house their cousin recommended was *really* Tudor till they learned it had no heating system, or that the village church was literally in the grounds, till she assured them of the deplorable uncertainty of the water-supply.

"It's too uncomfortable to be true!" Edward Boyne had continued to exult as the avowal of each disadvantage was successively wrung from her; but he had cut short his rhapsody to ask, with a relapse to distrust: "And the ghost? You've been concealing from us the fact that there is no ghost!"

Mary, at the moment, had laughed with him, yet almost with her laugh, being possessed of several sets of independent perceptions, had been struck by a note of flatness in Alida's answering hilarity.

"Oh, Dorsetshire's full of ghosts, you know."

"Yes, yes; but that won't do. I don't want to have to drive ten miles to see somebody else's ghost. I want one of my own on the premises. *Is* there a ghost at Lyng?"

His rejoinder had made Alida laugh again, and it was then that she had flung back tantalisingly: "Oh, there *is* one, of course, but you'll never know it."

"Never know it?" Boyne pulled her up. "But what in the world constitutes a ghost except the fact of its being known for one?"

"I can't say. But that's the story."

"That there's a ghost, but that nobody knows it's a ghost?"

"Well—not till afterward, at any rate."

"Till afterward?"

"Not till long, long afterward."

"But if it's once been identified as an unearthly visitant, why hasn't it *signalement* been handed down in the family? How has it managed to preserve its incognito?"

Alida could only shake her head. "Don't ask me. But it has."

"And then suddenly"—Mary spoke up as if from cavernous depths of divination—"suddenly, long afterward, one says to one's self '*That was* it?'"

She was startled at the sepulchral sound with which her question fell on the banter of the other two, and she saw the shadow of the same surprise flit across Alida's pupils. "I suppose so. One just has to wait."

"Oh, hang waiting!" Ned broke in. "Life's too short for a ghost who can only be enjoyed in retrospect. Can't we do better than that, Mary?"

But it turned out that in the event they were not destined to, for within three months of their conversation with Mrs. Stair they were settled at Lyng, and the life they had yearned for, to the point of planning it in advance in all its daily details, had actually begun for them.

It was to sit, in the thick December dusk, by just such a wide-hooded fireplace, under just such black oak rafters, with the sense that beyond the mullioned panes the downs were darkened to a deeper solitude: it was for the ultimate indulgence of such sensations that Mary Boyne, abruptly exiled from New York by her husband's business, had endured for nearly fourteen years the soul-deadening ugliness of a Middle Western town, and that Boyne had ground on doggedly at his engineering till, with a suddenness that still made her blink, the prodigious windfall of the Blue Star Mine had put them at a stroke in possession of life and the leisure to taste it. They had never for a moment meant their new state to be one of idleness; but they meant to give themselves only to harmonious activities. She had her vision of painting and gardening (against a background of grey walls), he dreamed of the production of his long-planned book on the "Economic Basis of Culture"; and with such absorbing work ahead no existence could be too sequestered: they could not get far enough from the world, or plunge deep enough into the past.

Dorsetshire had attracted them from the first by an air of remoteness out of all proportion to its geographical position. But to the Boynes it was one of the ever-recurring wonders of the whole incredibly compressed island—a nest of counties, as they put it—that for the production of its effects so little of a given quality went so far: that so few miles made a distance, and so short a distance a difference.

"It's that," Ned had once enthusiastically explained, "that gives such depth to their effects, such relief to their contrasts. They've been able to lay the butter so thick on every delicious mouthful."

The butter had certainly been laid on thick at Lyng: the old house hidden under a shoulder of the downs had almost all the finer marks of commerce with a protracted past. The mere fact that it was neither large nor exceptional made it, to the Boynes, abound the more completely in its special charm—the charm of having been for centuries a deep dim reservoir of life. The life had probably not been of the most vivid order: for long periods, no doubt, it had fallen as noiselessly into the past as the quiet drizzle of autumn fell, hour after hour, into the fish pond between the yews; but these back-waters of existence sometimes breed, in their sluggish depths, strange acuities of emotion, and Mary Boyne had felt from the first mysterious stir of intenser memories.

The feeling had never been stronger than on this particular afternoon when, waiting in the library for the lamps to come, she rose from her seat and stood among the shadows of the hearth. Her husband had gone off, after luncheon, for one of his long tramps on the downs. She had noticed of late that he preferred to go alone; and, in the tried security of their personal relations, had been driven to conclude that his book was bothering him, and that he needed the afternoons to turn over in solitude the problems left from the morning's work. Certainly the book was not going as smoothly as she had thought it would, and there were lines of perplexity between his eyes such as had never been there in his engineering days. He had often, then, looked fagged to the verge of illness, but the native demon of worry had never branded his brow. Yet the few pages he had so far read to her—the introduction, and a summary of the opening chapter—showed a firm hold on his subject, and an increasing confidence in his powers.

The fact threw her into deeper perplexity, since, now that he had done with "business" and its disturbing contingencies, the one other possible source of anxiety was eliminated. Unless it were his health, then? But physically he had gained since they had come to Dorsetshire, grown robuster, ruddier, and fresher-eyed. It was only within the last week that she had felt in him the undefinable change which made her restless in his absence, and as tongue-tied in his presence as though it were *she* who had a secret to keep from him!

The thought that there *was* a secret somewhere between them struck her with a sudden rap of wonder, and she looked about her down the long room.

"Can it be the house?" she mused.

The room itself might have been full of secrets. They seemed to be piling themselves up, as evening fell, like the layers and layers of velvet shadow dropping from the low ceiling, the rows of books, the smoke-blurred sculpture of the hearth.

"Why, of course—the house is haunted!" she reflected.

The ghost—Alida's imperceptible ghost—after figuring largely in the banter of their first month or two at Lyng, had been gradually left aside as too ineffectual for imaginative use. Mary had, indeed, as became the tenant of a haunted house, made the customary inquiries among her rural neighbours, but, beyond a vague "They do say so, Ma'am," the villagers had nothing to impart. The elusive spectre had apparently never had sufficient identity for a legend to crystallise about it, and after a time the Boynes had set the matter down to their profit-and-loss account, agreeing that Lyng was one of the few houses good enough in itself to dispense with supernatural enhancements.

"And I suppose, poor ineffectual demon, that's why it beats its beautiful wings in vain in the void," Mary had laughingly concluded.

"Or, rather," Ned answered in the same strain, "why, amid so much that's ghostly, it can never affirm its separate existence as *the* ghost." And thereupon their invisible housemate had finally dropped out of their references, which were numerous enough to make them soon unaware of the loss.

Now, as she stood on the hearth, the subject of their earlier curiosity revived in her with a new sense of its meaning—a sense gradually acquired through daily contact with the scene of the lurking mystery. It was the house itself, of course, that possessed the ghost-seeing faculty, that communed visually but secretly with its own past; if one could only get into close enough communion with the house, one might surprise its secret, and acquire the ghost-sight on one's own account. Perhaps, in his long hours in this very room, where she never trespassed till the afternoon, her husband *had* acquired it already, and was silently carrying about the weight of whatever it had revealed to him. Mary was too well versed in the code of the spectral world not to know that one could not talk about the ghosts one saw: to do so was almost as great a breach of taste as to name a lady in a club. But this explanation did not really satisfy her. "What, after all, except for the fun of the shudder," she reflected, "would he really care for any of their old ghosts?" And thence she was thrown back once more on the fundamental dilemma: the fact that one's greater or less susceptibility to spectral influences had no particular bearing on the case, since, when one *did* see a ghost at Lyng, one did not know it.

"Not till long afterward," Alida Stair had said. Well, supposing Ned *had* seen one when they first came, and had known only within the last week what had happened to him? More and more under the spell of the hour, she threw back her thoughts to the early days of their tenancy, but at first only to recall a lively confusion of unpacking, settling, arranging of books, and calling to each other from remote corners of the house as, treasure after treasure, it revealed itself to them. It was in this particular connection that she presently recalled a certain soft afternoon of the previous October, when, passing from the first rapturous flurry of exploration to a detailed inspection of the old house, she had pressed (like a novel heroine) a panel that opened on a flight of corkscrew stairs leading to a flat ledge of the roof—the roof which, from below, seemed to slope away on all sides too abruptly for any but practised feet to scale.

The view from this hidden coign was enchanting, and she had flown down to snatch Ned from his papers and give him the freedom of her discovery. She remembered still how, standing at her side, he had passed his arm about her while their gaze flew to the long tossed horizon-line of the downs, and then dropped contentedly back to trace the arabesque of yew hedges about the fish-pond, and the shadow of the cedar on the lawn.

"And now the other way," he had said, turning her about within his arm; and closely pressed to him, she had absorbed, like some long satisfying draught, the picture of the grey-walled court, the squat lions on the gates, and the lime-avenue reaching up to the high-road under the downs.

It was just then, while they gazed and held each other, that she had felt his arm relax, and heard a sharp "Hullo!" that made her turn to glance at him.

Distinctly, yes, she now recalled that she had seen, as she glanced, a shadow of anxiety, of perplexity, rather, fall across his face; and, following his eyes, had beheld the figure of a man—a man in loose greyish clothes, as it appeared to her—who was sauntering down the lime-avenue to the court with the doubtful gait of a stranger who seeks his way. Her short-sighted eyes had given her but a blurred impression of slightness and greyishness, with something foreign, or at least unlocal, in the cut of the figure or its dress; but her husband had apparently seen more—seen enough to make him push past her with a hasty "Wait!" and dash down the stairs without pausing to give her a hand.

A slight tendency to dizziness obliged her, after a provisional clutch at the chimney against which they had been leaning, to follow him first more cautiously; and when she had reached the landing she paused again, for a less definite reason, leaning over the banister to strain her eyes through the silence of the brown sun-flecked depths. She lingered there till, somewhere in those depths, she heard the closing of a door; then, mechanically impelled, she went down the shallow flights of steps till she reached the lower hall.

The front door stood open on the sunlight of the court, and hall and court were empty. The library door was open, too, and after listening in vain for any sound of voices within, she crossed the threshold, and found her husband alone, vaguely fingering the papers on his desk.

He looked up, as if surprised at her entrance, but the shadow of anxiety had passed from his face, leaving it even, as she fancied, a little brighter and clearer than usual.

"What was it? Who was it?" she asked.

"Who?" he repeated, with the surprise still all on his side.

"The man we saw coming toward the house."

He seemed to reflect. "The man? Why, I thought I saw Peters; I dashed after him to say a word about the stable drains, but he had disappeared before I could get down."

"Disappeared? But he seemed to be walking so slowly when we saw him."

Boyne shrugged his shoulders. "So I thought; but he must have got up steam in the interval. What do you say to our trying a scramble up Meldon Steep before sunset?"

That was all. At the time the occurrence had been less than nothing, had, indeed, been immediately obliterated by the magic of their first vision from Meldon Steep, a height which they had dreamed of climbing ever since they had first seen its bare spine rising above the roof of Lyng. Doubtless it was the mere fact of the other incident's having occurred on the very day of their ascent to Meldon that had kept it stored away in the fold of memory from which it now emerged; for in itself it had no mark of the portentous. At the moment there could have been nothing more natural than that Ned should dash himself from the roof in the pursuit of dilatory tradesmen. It was the period when they were always on the watch for one or the other of the specialists employed about the place; always lying in wait for them, and rushing out at them with questions, reproaches, or reminders. And certainly in the distance the grey figure had looked like Peters.

Yet now, as she reviewed the scene, she felt her husband's explanation of it to have been invalidated by the look of anxiety on his face. Why had the familiar appearance of Peters made him anxious? Why, above all, if it was of such prime necessity to confer with him on the subject of the stable drains, had the failure to find him produced such a look of relief? Mary could not say that any one of these questions had occurred to her at the time, yet, from the promptness with which they now marshalled themselves at her summons, she had a sense that they must all along have been there, waiting their hour.

II

Weary with her thoughts, she moved to the window. The library was now quite dark, and she was surprised to see how much faint light the outer world still held.

As she peered out into it across the court, a figure shaped itself far down the perspective of bare limes: it looked a mere blot of deeper grey in the greyness, and for an instant, as it moved toward her, her heart thumped to the thought "It's the ghost!"

She had time, in that long instant, to feel suddenly that the man of whom, two months earlier, she had had a distant vision from the roof, was now, at his predestined hour, about to reveal himself as *not* having been Peters; and her spirit sank under the impending fear of the disclosure. But almost with the next tick of the clock the figure, gaining substance and character, showed itself even to her weak sight as her husband's; and she turned to meet him, as he entered, with the confession of her folly.

"It's really too absurd," she laughed out, "but I never *can* remember!"

"Remember what?" Boyne questioned as they drew together.

"That when one sees the Lyng ghost one never knows it."

Her hand was on his sleeve, and he kept it there, but with no response in his gesture or in the lines of his preoccupied face.

"Did you think you'd seen it?" he asked, after an appreciable interval.

"Why, I actually took *you* for it, my dear, in my mad determination to spot it!"

"Me—just now?" His arm dropped away, and he turned from her with a faint echo of her laugh. "Really, dearest, you'd better give it up, if that's the best you can do."

"Oh, yes, I give it up. Have *you?*" she asked, turning round on him abruptly.

The parlour-maid had entered with letters and a lamp, and the light struck up into Boyne's face as he bent above the tray she presented.

"Have *you?*" Mary perversely insisted, when the servant had disappeared on her errand of illumination.

"Have I what?" he rejoined absently, the light bringing out the sharp stamp of worry between his brows as he turned over the letters.

"Given up trying to see the ghost." Her heart beat a little at the experiment she was making.

Her husband, laying his letters aside, moved away into the shadow of the hearth.

"I never tried," he said, tearing open the wrapper of a newspaper.

"Well, of course," Mary persisted, "the exasperating thing is that there's no use trying, since one can't be sure till so long afterward."

He was unfolding the paper as if he had hardly heard her; but after a pause, during which the sheets rustled spasmodically between his hands, he looked up to ask, "Have you any idea *how long?*"

Mary had sunk into a low chair beside the fireplace. From her seat she glanced over, startled, at her husband's profile, which was projected against the circle of lamplight.

"No; none. Have *you?*" she retorted, repeating her former phrase with an added stress of intention.

Boyne crumpled the paper into a bunch, and then, inconsequently, turned back with it toward the lamp.

"Lord, no! I only meant," he exclaimed, with a faint tinge of impatience, "is there any legend, any tradition, as to that?"

"Not that I know of," she answered; but the impulse to add "What makes you ask?" was checked by the reappearance of the parlour-maid, with tea and a second lamp.

With the dispersal of shadows, and the repetition of the daily domestic office, Mary Boyne felt herself less oppressed by that sense of something mutely imminent which had darkened her afternoon. For a few moments she gave herself to the details of her task, and when she looked up from it she was struck to the point of bewilderment by the change in her husband's face. He had seated himself near the farther lamp, and was absorbed in the perusal of his letters; but was it something he had found in them, or merely the shifting of her own point of view, that had restored his features to their normal aspect? The longer she looked the more definitely the change affirmed itself. The lines of tension had vanished, and such traces of fatigue as lingered were of the kind easily attributable to steady mental effort. He glanced up, as if drawn by her gaze, and met her eyes with a smile.

"I'm dying for my tea, you know; and here's a letter for you," he said.

She took the letter he held out in exchange for the cup she proffered him, and, returning to her seat, broke the seal with the languid gesture of the reader whose interests are all enclosed in the circle of one cherished presence.

Her next conscious motion was that of starting to her feet, the letter falling to them as she rose, while she held out to her husband a newspaper clipping.

"Ned! What's this? What does it mean?"

He had risen at the same instant, almost as if hearing her cry before she uttered it; and for a perceptible space of time he and she studied each other, like adversaries watching for an advantage, across the space between her chair and his desk.

"What's that? You fairly made me jump!" Boyne said at length, moving toward her with a sudden half-exasperated laugh. The shadow of apprehension was on his face again, not now a look of fixed foreboding, but a shifting vigilance of lips and eyes that gave her the sense of his feeling himself invisibly surrounded.

Her hand shook so that she could hardly give him the clipping.

"This article—from the *Waukesha Sentinel*—that a man named Elwell has brought suit against you—that there was something wrong about the Blue Star Mine. I can't understand more than half."

They continued to face each other as she spoke, and to her astonishment she saw that her words had the almost immediate effect of dissipating the strained watchfulness of his look.

"Oh, *that!*" He glanced down the printed slip, and then folded it with the gesture of one who handles something harmless and familiar. "What's the matter with you this afternoon, Mary? I thought you'd got bad news."

She stood before him with her undefinable terror subsiding slowly under the reassurance of his tone.

"You knew about this, then—it's all right?"

"Certainly I knew about it; and it's all right."

"But what *is* it? I don't understand. What does this man accuse you of?"

"Pretty nearly every crime in the calendar." Boyne had tossed the clipping down, and thrown himself into an armchair near the fire. "Do you want to hear the story? It's not particularly interesting—just a squabble over interests in the Blue Star."

"But who is this Elwell? I don't know the name."

"Oh, he's a fellow I put into it—gave him a hand up. I told you all about him at the time."

"I dare say. I must have forgotten." Vainly she strained back among her memories. "But if you helped him, why does he make this return?"

"Probably some shyster lawyer got hold of him and talked him over. It's all rather technical and complicated. I thought that kind of thing bored you."

His wife felt a sting of compunction. Theoretically, she deprecated the American wife's detachment from her husband's professional interests, but in practice she had always found it difficult to fix her attention on Boyne's report of the transactions in which his varied interests involved him. Besides, she had felt during their years of exile, that, in a community where the amenities of living could be obtained only at the cost of efforts as arduous as her husband's professional labour, such brief leisure as he and she could command should be used as an escape from immediate preoccupations, a flight to the life they always dreamed of living. Once or twice, now that this new life had actually drawn its magic circle about them, she had asked herself if she had done right; but hitherto such conjectures had been no more than the retrospective excursions of an active fancy. Now, for the first time, it startled her a little to find how little she knew of the material foundation on which her happiness was built.

She glanced at her husband, and was again reassured by the composure of his face; yet she felt the need of more definite grounds for her reassurance.

"But doesn't this suit worry you? Why have you never spoken to me about it?"

He answered both questions at once. "I didn't speak of it at first because it *did* worry me—annoyed me, rather. But it's all ancient history now. Your correspondent must have got hold of a back number of the *Sentinel*."

She felt a quick thrill of relief. "You mean it's over? He's lost his case?"

There was a just perceptible delay in Boyne's reply. "The suit's been withdrawn—that's all."

But she persisted, as if to exonerate herself from the inward charge of being too easily put off. "Withdrawn it because he saw he had no chance?"

"Oh, he had no chance," Boyne answered.

She was still struggling with a dimly felt perplexity at the back of her thoughts.

"How long ago was it withdrawn?"

He paused, as if with a slight return to his former uncertainty. "I've just had the news now; but I've been expecting it."

"Just now—in one of your letters?"

"Yes; in one of my letters."

She made no answer, and was aware only, after a short interval of waiting, that he had risen, and, strolling across the room, had placed himself on the sofa at her side. She felt him, as he did so, pass an arm about her, she felt his hand seek hers and clasp it, and turning slowly, drawn by the warmth of his cheek, she met his smiling eyes.

"It's all right—it's all right?" she questioned, through the flood of her dissolving doubts; and "I give you my word it was never righter!" he laughed back at her, holding her close.

III

One of the strangest things she was afterward to recall out of all the next day's strangeness was the sudden and complete recovery of her sense of security.

It was in the air when she woke in her low-ceiled, dusky room; it went with her downstairs to the breakfast-table, flashed out at her from the fire, and reduplicated itself from the flanks of the urn and the sturdy flutings of the Georgian teapot. It was as if, in some roundabout way, all her diffused fears of the previous day, with their moment of sharp concentration about the newspaper article—as if this dim questioning of the future, and startled return upon the past, had between them liquidated the arrears of some haunting moral obligation. If she had indeed been careless of her husband's affairs, it was, her new state seemed to prove, because her faith in him instinctively justified such carelessness; and his right to her faith had now affirmed itself in the very face of menace and suspicion. She had never seen him more untroubled, more naturally and unconsciously himself, than after the cross-examination to

which she had subjected him: it was almost as if he had been aware
of her doubts, and had wanted the air cleared as much as she did.

It was as clear, thank heaven, as the bright outer light that surprised her almost with a touch of summer when she issued from
the house for her daily round of the gardens. She had left Boyne
at his desk, indulging herself, as she passed the library door, by a
last peep at his quiet face, where he bent, pipe in mouth, about his
papers; and now she had her own morning's task to perform. The
task involved, on such charmed winter days, almost as much happy
loitering about the different quarters of her demesne as if spring
were already at work there. There were such endless possibilities
still before her, such opportunities to bring out the latent graces
of the old place, without a single irreverent touch of alteration,
that the winter was all too short to plan what spring and autumn
executed. And her recovered sense of safety gave, on this particular
morning, a peculiar zest to her progress through the sweet, still
place. She went first to the kitchen garden, where the espaliered
pear trees drew complicated patterns on the walls, and pigeons
were fluttering and preening about the silvery-slated roof of their
cot. There was something wrong about the piping of the hothouse,
and she was expecting an authority from Dorchester, who was to
drive out between trains and make a diagnosis of the boiler. But
when she dipped into the damp heat of the greenhouses, among
the spiced scents and waxy pinks and reds of old-fashioned exot-
ics—even the flora of Lyng was in the note!—she learned that the
great man had not arrived, and, the day being too rare to waste
in an artificial atmosphere, she came out again and paced along
the springy turf of the bowling-green to the gardens behind the
house. At their farther end rose a grass terrace, looking across the
fish-pond and yew hedges to the long house-front with its twisted

chimney-stacks and blue roof angles all drenched in the pale gold moisture of the air.

Seen thus, across the level tracery of the gardens, it sent her, from open windows and hospitably smoking chimneys, the look of some warm human presence, of a mind slowly ripened on a sunny wall of experience. She had never before had such a sense of her intimacy with it, such a conviction that its secrets were all beneficent, kept, as they said to children, "for one's good", such a trust in its power to gather up her life and Ned's into the harmonious pattern of the long, long story it sat there weaving in the sun.

She heard steps behind her, and turned, expecting to see the gardener accompanied by the engineer from Dorchester. But only one figure was in sight, that of a youngish, slightly built man, who, for reasons she could not on the spot have given, did not remotely resemble her notion of an authority on hothouse boilers. The new-comer, on seeing her, lifted his hat, and paused with the air of a gentleman—perhaps a traveller—who wishes to make it known that his intrusion is involuntary. Lyng occasionally attracted the more cultivated sight-seer, and Mary half-expected to see the stranger dissemble a camera, or justify his presence by producing it. But he made no gesture of any sort, and after a moment she asked, in a tone responding to the courteous hesitation of his attitude: "Is there anyone you wish to see?"

"I came to see Mr. Boyne," he answered. His intonation, rather than his accent, was faintly American, and Mary, at the note, looked at him more closely. The brim of his soft felt hat cast a shade on his face, which, thus obscured, wore to her short-sighted gaze a look of seriousness, as of a person arriving on business, and civilly but firmly aware of his rights.

Past experience had made her equally sensible to such claims; but she was jealous of her husband's morning hours, and doubtful of his having given anyone the right to intrude on them.

"Have you an appointment with my husband?" she asked.

The visitor hesitated, as if unprepared for the question.

"I think he expects me," he replied.

It was Mary's turn to hesitate. "You see this is his time for work: he never sees anyone in the morning."

He looked at her a moment without answering; then, as if accepting her decision, he began to move away. As he turned, Mary saw him pause and glance up at the peaceful house front. Something in his air suggested weariness and disappointment, the dejection of the traveller who has come from far off and whose hours are limited by the timetable. It occurred to her that if this were the case her refusal might have made his errand vain, and a sense of compunction caused her to hasten after him.

"May I ask if you have come a long way?"

He gave her the same grave look. "Yes—I have come a long way."

"Then, if you'll go to the house, no doubt my husband will see you now. You'll find him in the library."

She did not know why she had added the last phrase, except from a vague impulse to atone for her previous inhospitality. The visitor seemed about to express his thanks, but her attention was distracted by the approach of the gardener with a companion who bore all the marks of being the expert from Dorchester.

"This way," she said, waving the stranger to the house; and an instant later she had forgotten him in the absorption of her meeting with the boiler-maker.

The encounter led to such far-reaching results that the engineer ended by finding it expedient to ignore his train, and Mary was beguiled into spending the remainder of the morning in absorbed confabulation among the flower pots. When the colloquy ended, she was surprised to find that it was nearly luncheon time, and she half expected, as she hurried back to the house, to see her husband coming out to meet her. But she found no one in the court but an undergardener raking the gravel, and the hall, when she entered it, was so silent that she guessed Boyne to be still at work.

Not wishing to disturb him, she turned into the drawing room, and there, at her writing table, lost herself in renewed calculations of the outlay to which the morning's conference had pledged her. The fact that she could permit herself such follies had not yet lost its novelty; and somehow, in contrast to the vague fears of the previous days, it now seemed an element of her recovered security, of the sense that, as Ned had said, things in general had never been "righter".

She was still luxuriating in a lavish play of figures when the parlourmaid, from the threshold, roused her with an inquiry as to the expediency of serving luncheon. It was one of their jokes that Trimmle announced luncheon as if she were divulging a state secret, and Mary, intent upon her papers, merely murmured an absent-minded assent.

She felt Trimmle wavering doubtfully on the threshold, as if in rebuke of such unconsidered assent; then her retreating steps sounded down the passage, and Mary, pushing away her papers, crossed the hall and went to the library door. It was still closed, and she wavered in her turn, disliking to disturb her husband, yet anxious that he should not exceed his usual measure of work. As she stood there, balancing her impulses, Trimmle returned with the announcement of luncheon, and Mary, thus impelled, opened the library door.

Boyne was not at his desk, and she peered about her, expecting to discover him before the book-shelves, somewhere down the length of the room; but her call brought no response, and gradually it became clear to her that he was not there.

She turned back to the parlour-maid.

"Mr. Boyne must be upstairs. Please tell him that luncheon is ready."

Trimmle appeared to hesitate between the obvious duty of obedience and an equally obvious conviction of the foolishness of the injunction laid on her. The struggle resulted in her saying: "If you please, madam, Mr. Boyne's not upstairs."

"Not in his room? Are you sure?"

"I'm sure, madam."

Mary consulted the clock. "Where is he, then?"

"He's gone out," Trimmle announced, with the superior air of one who has respectfully waited for the question that a well-ordered mind would have put first.

Mary's conjecture had been right, then. Boyne must have gone to the gardens to meet her, and since she had missed him, it was clear that he had taken the shorter way by the south door, instead of going round to the court. She crossed the hall to the French window opening directly on the yew garden, but the parlour-maid, after another moment of inner conflict, decided to bring out: "Please, madam, Mr. Boyne didn't go that way."

Mary turned back. "Where *did* he go? And when?"

"He went out of the front door, up the drive, madam." It was a matter of principle with Trimmle never to answer more than one question at a time.

"Up the drive? At this hour?" Mary went to the door herself, and glanced across the court through the tunnel of bare limes.

But its perspective was as empty as when she had scanned it on entering.

"Did Mr. Boyne leave no message?"

Trimmle seemed to surrender herself to a last struggle with the forces of chaos.

"No, madam. He just went out with the gentleman."

"The gentleman? What gentleman?" Mary wheeled about, as if to front this new factor.

"The gentleman who called, madam," said Trimmle resignedly.

"When did a gentleman call? Do explain yourself, Trimmle!"

Only the fact that Mary was very hungry, and that she wanted to consult her husband about the greenhouses, would have caused her to lay so unusual an injunction on her attendant; and even now she was detached enough to note in Trimmle's eye the dawning defiance of the respectful subordinate who has been pressed too hard.

"I couldn't exactly say the hour, madam, because I didn't let the gentleman in," she replied, with an air of discreetly ignoring the irregularity of her mistress's course.

"You didn't let him in?"

"No, madam. When the bell rang I was dressing, and Agnes—"

"Go and ask Agnes, then," said Mary.

Trimmle still wore her look of patient magnanimity. "Agnes would not know, madam, for she had unfortunately burnt her hand in trimming the wick of the new lamp from town"—Trimmle, as Mary was aware, had always been opposed to the new lamp—"and so Mrs. Dockett sent the kitchen-maid instead."

Mary looked again at the clock. "It's after two! Go and ask the kitchen-maid if Mr. Boyne left any word."

She went into luncheon without waiting, and Trimmle presently brought her there the kitchen-maid's statement that the gentleman had called about eleven o'clock, and that Mr. Boyne had gone out with him without leaving any message. The kitchen-maid did not even know the caller's name, for he had written it on a slip of paper, which he had folded and handed to her, with the injunction to deliver it at once to Mr. Boyne.

Mary finished her luncheon, still wondering, and when it was over, and Trimmle had brought the coffee to the drawing room, her wonder had deepened to a first faint tinge of disquietude. It was unlike Boyne to absent himself without explanation at so unwonted an hour, and the difficulty of identifying the visitor whose summons he had apparently obeyed made his disappearance the more unaccountable. Mary Boyne's experience as the wife of a busy engineer, subject to sudden calls and compelled to keep irregular hours, had trained her to the philosophic acceptance of surprises; but since Boyne's withdrawal from business he had adopted a Benedictine regularity of life. As if to make up for the dispersed and agitated years, with their "stand-up" lunches, and dinners rattled down to the joltings of the dining-cars, he cultivated the last refinements of punctuality and monotony, discouraging his wife's fancy for the unexpected, and declaring that to a delicate taste there were infinite gradations of pleasure in the recurrences of habit.

Still, since no life can completely defend itself from the unforeseen, it was evident that all Boyne's precautions would sooner or later prove unavailable, and Mary concluded that he had cut short a tiresome visit by walking with his caller to the station, or at least accompanying him for part of the way.

This conclusion relieved her from further preoccupation, and she went out herself to take up her conference with the gardener. Thence she walked to the village post office, a mile or so away; and when she turned toward home the early twilight was setting in.

She had taken a footpath across the downs, and as Boyne, meanwhile, had probably returned from the station by the high road, there was little likelihood of their meeting. She felt sure, however, of his having reached the house before her; so sure that, when she entered it herself, without even pausing to inquire of Trimmle, she made directly for the library. But the library was still empty, and with an unwonted exactness of visual memory she observed that the papers on her husband's desk lay precisely as they had lain when she had gone in to call him to luncheon.

Then of a sudden she was seized by a vague dread of the unknown. She had closed the door behind her on entering, and as she stood alone in the long, silent room, her dread seemed to take shape and sound, to be there breathing and lurking among the shadows. Her short-sighted eyes strained through them, half-discerning an actual presence, something aloof, that watched and knew; and in the recoil from that intangible presence she threw herself on the bell-rope and gave it a sharp pull.

The sharp summons brought Trimmle in precipitately with a lamp, and Mary breathed again at this sobering reappearance of the usual.

"You may bring tea if Mr. Boyne is in," she said, to justify her ring.

"Very well, madam. But Mr. Boyne is not in," said Trimmle, putting down the lamp.

"Not in? You mean he's come back and gone out again?"

"No, madam. He's never been back."

The dread stirred again, and Mary knew that now it had her fast.

"Not since he went out with—the gentleman?"

"Not since he went out with the gentleman."

"But who *was* the gentleman?" Mary insisted, with the shrill note of someone trying to be heard through a confusion of noises.

"That I couldn't say, madam." Trimmle, standing there by the lamp, seemed suddenly to grow less round and rosy, as though eclipsed by the same creeping shade of apprehension.

"But the kitchen-maid knows—wasn't it the kitchen-maid who let him in?"

"She doesn't know either, madam, for he wrote his name on a folded paper."

Mary, through her agitation, was aware that they were both designating the unknown visitor by a vague pronoun, instead of the conventional formula which, till then, had kept their allusions within the bounds of conformity. And at the same moment her mind caught at the suggestion of the folded paper.

"But he must have a name! Where's the paper?"

She moved to the desk, and began to turn over the documents that littered it. The first that caught her eye was an unfinished letter in her husband's hand, with his pen lying across it, as though dropped there at a sudden summons.

"My dear Parvis"—who was Parvis?—*"I have just received your letter announcing Elwell's death, and while I suppose there is now no further risk of trouble, it might be safer—"*

She tossed the sheet aside, and continued her search; but no folded paper was discoverable among the letters and pages of manuscript which had been swept together in a heap, as if by a hurried or a startled gesture.

"But the kitchen-maid *saw* him. Send her here," she commanded, wondering at her dullness in not thinking sooner of so simple a solution.

Trimmle vanished in a flash, as if thankful to be out of the room, and when she reappeared, conducting the agitated underling, Mary had regained her self-possession, and had her questions ready.

The gentleman was a stranger, yes—that she understood. But what had he said? And, above all, what had he looked like? The first question was easily enough answered, for the disconcerting reason that he had said so little—had merely asked for Mr. Boyne, and, scribbling something on a bit of paper, had requested that it should at once be carried in to him.

"Then you don't know what he wrote? You're not sure it *was* his name?"

The kitchen-maid was not sure, but supposed it was, since he had written it in answer to her inquiry as to whom she should announce.

"And when you carried the paper in to Mr. Boyne, what did he say?"

The kitchen-maid did not think that Mr. Boyne had said anything, but she could not be sure, for just as she had handed him the paper and he was opening it, she had become aware that the visitor had followed her into the library, and she had slipped out, leaving the two gentlemen together.

"But then, if you left them in the library, how do you know that they went out of the house?"

This question plunged the witness into a momentary inarticulateness, from which she was rescued by Trimmle, who, by means of ingenious circumlocutions, elicited the statement that before she could cross the hall to the back passage she had heard the two gentlemen behind her, and had seen them go out of the front door together.

"Then, if you saw the strange gentleman twice, you must be able to tell me what he looked like."

But with this final challenge to her powers of expression it became clear that the limit of the kitchen-maid's endurance had been reached. The obligation of going to the front door to "show in" a visitor was in itself so subversive of the fundamental order of things that it had thrown her faculties into hopeless disarray, and she could only stammer out, after various panting efforts: "His hat, mum, was different-like, as you might say—"

"Different? How different?" Mary flashed out, her own mind, in the same instant, leaping back to an image left on it that morning, and then lost under layers of subsequent impressions.

"His hat had a wide brim, you mean, and his face was pale—a youngish face?" Mary pressed her, with a white-lipped intensity of interrogation. But if the kitchen-maid found any adequate answer to this challenge, it was swept away for her listener down the rushing current of her own convictions. The stranger—the stranger in the garden! Why had Mary not thought of him before? She needed no one now to tell her that it was he who had called for her husband and gone away with him. But who was he, and why had Boyne obeyed him?

IV

It leaped out at her suddenly, like a grin out of the dark, that they had often called England so little—"such a confoundedly hard place to get lost in".

A confoundedly hard place to get lost in! That had been her husband's phrase. And now, with the whole machinery of official investigation sweeping its flashlights from shore to shore, and across the dividing straits; now, with Boyne's name blazing from the walls of every town and village, his portrait (how that wrung her!) hawked up and down the country like the image of a hunted criminal; now the little compact populous island, so policed, surveyed, and administered, revealed itself as a Sphinx-like guardian of abysmal mysteries, staring back into his wife's anguished eyes as if with the wicked joy of knowing something they would never know!

In the fortnight since Boyne's disappearance there had been no word of him, no trace of his movements. Even the usual misleading reports that raise expectancy in tortured bosoms had been few and fleeting. No one but the kitchen-maid had seen Boyne leave the house, and no one else had seen "the gentleman" who accompanied him. All inquiries in the neighbourhood failed to elicit the memory of a stranger's presence that day in the neighbourhood of Lyng. And no one had met Edward Boyne, either alone or in company, in any of the neighbouring villages, or on the road across the downs, or at either of the local railway stations. The sunny English noon had swallowed him as completely as if he had gone out into Cimmerian night.

Mary, while every official means of investigation was working at its highest pressure, had ransacked her husband's papers for any trace of antecedent complications, of entanglements or obligations unknown to her, that might throw a ray into the darkness. But if any such had existed in the background of Boyne's life, they had vanished like the slip of paper on which the visitor had written his name. There remained no possible thread of guidance except—if it were indeed an exception—the letter which Boyne had apparently been in the act of writing when he received his mysterious summons. That letter, read and re-read by his wife, and submitted by her to the police, yielded little enough to feed conjecture.

"I have just heard of Elwell's death, and while I suppose there is now no further risk of trouble, it might be safer—" That was all. The "risk of trouble" was easily explained by the newspaper clipping which had apprised Mary of the suit brought against her husband by one of his associates in the Blue Star enterprise. The only new information conveyed by the letter was the fact of its showing Boyne, when he wrote it, to be still apprehensive of the results of the suit, though he had told his wife that it had been withdrawn, and though the letter itself proved that the plaintiff was dead. It took several days of cabling to fix the identity of the "Parvis" to whom the fragment was addressed, but even after these inquiries had shown him to be a Waukesha lawyer, no new facts concerning the Elwell suit were elicited. He appeared to have had no direct concern in it, but to have been conversant with the facts merely as an acquaintance, and possible intermediary; and he declared himself unable to guess with what object Boyne intended to seek his assistance.

This negative information, sole fruit of the first fortnight's search, was not increased by a jot during the slow weeks that followed. Mary knew that the investigations were still being carried on, but she had a vague sense of their gradually slackening, as the actual march of time seemed to slacken. It was as though the days, flying horror-struck from the shrouded image of the one inscrutable day, gained assurance as the distance lengthened, till at last they fell back into their normal gait. And so with the human imaginations at work on the dark event. No doubt it occupied them still, but week by week and hour by hour it grew less absorbing, took up less space, was slowly but inevitably crowded out of the foreground of consciousness by the new problems perpetually bubbling up from the cloudy caldron of human experience.

Even Mary Boyne's consciousness gradually felt the same lowering of velocity. It still swayed with the incessant oscillations of conjecture; but they were slower, more rhythmical in their beat. There were even moments of weariness when, like the victim of some poison which leaves the brain clear, but holds the body motionless, she saw herself domesticated with the Horror, accepting its perpetual presence as one of the fixed conditions of life.

These moments lengthened into hours and days, till she passed into a phase of stolid acquiescence. She watched the routine of daily life with the incurious eye of a savage on whom the meaningless processes of civilisation make but the faintest impression. She had come to regard herself as part of the routine, a spoke of the wheel, revolving with its motion; she felt almost like the furniture of the room in which she sat, an insensate object to be dusted and pushed about with the chairs and tables. And this deepening apathy held her fast at Lyng, in spite of the entreaties of friends and the usual medical recommendation of "change". Her friends supposed that her refusal to move was inspired by the belief that her husband would one day return to the spot from which he had vanished, and a beautiful legend grew up about this imaginary state of waiting. But in reality she had no such belief: the depths of anguish enclosing her were no longer lighted by flashes of hope. She was sure that Boyne would never come back, that he had gone out of her sight as completely as if Death itself had waited that day on the threshold. She had even renounced, one by one, the various theories as to his disappearance which had been advanced by the press, the police, and her own agonised imagination. In sheer lassitude her mind turned from these alternatives of horror, and sank back into the blank fact that he was gone.

No, she would never know what had become of him—no one would ever know. But the house *knew*; the library in which she spent her long, lonely evenings knew. For it was here that the last scene had been enacted, here that the stranger had come and spoken the word which had caused Boyne to rise and follow him. The floor she trod had felt his tread; the books on the shelves had seen his face; and there were moments when the intense consciousness of the old dusky walls seemed about to break out into some audible revelation of their secret. But the revelation never came, and she knew it would never come. Lyng was not one of the garrulous old houses that betray the secrets entrusted to them. Its very legend proved that it had always been the mute accomplice, the incorruptible custodian, of the mysteries it had surprised. And Mary Boyne, sitting face to face with its silence, felt the futility of seeking to break it by any human means.

v

"I don't say it *wasn't* straight, and yet I don't say it *was* straight. It was business."

Mary, at the words, lifted her head with a start, and looked intently at the speaker.

When, half an hour before, a card with "Mr. Parvis" on it had been brought up to her, she had been immediately aware that the name had been a part of her consciousness ever since she had read it at the head of Boyne's unfinished letter. In the library she had found awaiting her a small sallow man with a bald head and gold eye-glasses, and it sent a tremor through her to know that this was the person to whom her husband's last known thought had been directed.

Parvis, civilly, but without vain preamble—in the manner of a man who has his watch in his hand—had set forth the object of his visit. He had "run over" to England on business, and finding himself in the neighbourhood of Dorchester, had not wished to leave it without paying his respects to Mrs. Boyne; and without asking her, if the occasion offered, what she meant to do about Bob Elwell's family.

The words touched the spring of some obscure dread in Mary's bosom. Did her visitor, after all, know what Boyne had meant by his unfinished phrase? She asked for an elucidation of his question, and noticed at once that he seemed surprised at her continued ignorance of the subject. Was it possible that she really knew as little as she said?

"I know nothing—you must tell me," she faltered out; and her visitor thereupon proceeded to unfold his story. It threw, even to her confused perceptions and imperfectly initiated vision, a lurid glare on the whole hazy episode of the Blue Star Mine. Her husband had made his money in that brilliant speculation at the cost of "getting ahead" of someone less alert to seize the chance; and the victim of his ingenuity was young Robert Elwell, who had "put him on" to the Blue Star scheme.

Parvis, at Mary's first cry, had thrown her a sobering glance through his impartial glasses.

"Bob Elwell wasn't smart enough, that's all; if he had been, he might have turned round and served Boyne the same way. It's the kind of thing that happens every day in business. I guess it's what the scientists call the survival of the fittest—see?" said Mr. Parvis, evidently pleased with the aptness of his analogy.

Mary felt a physical shrinking from the next question she tried to frame: it was as though the words on her lips had a taste that nauseated her.

"But then—you accuse my husband of doing something dishonourable?"

Mr. Parvis surveyed the question dispassionately. "Oh, no, I don't. I don't even say it wasn't straight." He glanced up and down the long lines of books, as if one of them might have supplied him with the definition he sought. "I don't say it *wasn't* straight, and yet I don't say it *was* straight. It was business." After all, no definition in his category could be more comprehensive than that.

Mary sat staring at him with a look of terror. He seemed to her like the indifferent emissary of some evil power.

"But Mr. Elwell's lawyers apparently did not take your view, since I suppose the suit was withdrawn by their advice."

"Oh, yes; they knew he hadn't a leg to stand on, technically. It was when they advised him to withdraw the suit that he got desperate. You see, he'd borrowed most of the money he lost in the Blue Star, and he was up a tree. That's why he shot himself when they told him he had no show."

The horror was sweeping over Mary in great deafening waves.

"He shot himself? He killed himself because of *that*?"

"Well, he didn't kill himself, exactly. He dragged on two months before he died." Parvis emitted the statement as unemotionally as a gramophone grinding out its "record".

"You mean that he tried to kill himself, and failed? And tried again?"

"Oh, he didn't have to *try* again," said Parvis grimly.

They sat opposite each other in silence, he swinging his eye-glasses thoughtfully about his finger, she, motionless, her arms stretched along her knees in an attitude of rigid tension.

"But if you knew all this," she began at length, hardly able to force her voice above a whisper, "how is it that when I wrote you at the time of my husband's disappearance you said you didn't understand his letter?"

Parvis received this without perceptible embarrassment: "Why, I didn't understand it—strictly speaking. And it wasn't the time to talk about it, if I had. The Elwell business was settled when the suit was withdrawn. Nothing I could have told you would have helped you to find your husband."

Mary continued to scrutinise him. "Then why are you telling me now?"

Still Parvis did not hesitate. "Well, to begin with, I supposed you knew more than you appear to—I mean about the circumstances of Elwell's death. And then people are talking of it now; the whole matter's been raked up again. And I thought if you didn't know you ought to."

She remained silent, and he continued: "You see, it's only come out lately what a bad state Elwell's affairs were in. His wife's a proud woman, and she fought on as long as she could, going out to work, and taking sewing at home when she got too sick—something with the heart, I believe. But she had his mother to look after, and the children, and she broke down under it, and finally had to ask for help. That called attention to the case, and the papers took it up, and a subscription was started. Everybody out there liked Bob Elwell, and most of the prominent names in the place are down on the list, and people began to wonder why—"

Parvis broke off to fumble in an inner pocket. "Here," he continued, "here's an account of the whole thing from the *Sentinel*—a little sensational, of course. But I guess you'd better look it over."

He held out a newspaper to Mary, who unfolded it slowly, remembering, as she did so, the evening when, in that same room, the perusal of a clipping from the *Sentinel* had first shaken the depths of her security.

As she opened the paper, her eyes, shrinking from the glaring headlines, "Widow of Boyne's Victim Forced to Appeal for Aid," ran down the column of text to two portraits inserted in it. The first was her husband's, taken from a photograph made the year they had come to England. It was the picture of him that she liked best, the one that stood on the writing-table upstairs in her bedroom. As the eyes in the photograph met hers, she felt it would be impossible to read what was said of him, and closed her lids with the sharpness of the pain.

"I thought if you felt disposed to put your name down—" she heard Parvis continue.

She opened her eyes with an effort, and they fell on the other portrait. It was that of a youngish man, slightly built, with features somewhat blurred by the shadow of a projecting hat-brim. Where had she seen that outline before? She stared at it confusedly, her heart hammering in her ears. Then she gave a cry.

"This is the man—the man who came for my husband!"

She heard Parvis start to his feet, and was dimly aware that she had slipped backward into the corner of the sofa, and that he was bending above her in alarm. She straightened herself, and reached out for the paper, which she had dropped.

"It's the man! I should know him anywhere!" she persisted in a voice that sounded to her own ears like a scream.

Parvis's answer seemed to come to her from far off, down endless fog-muffled windings.

"Mrs. Boyne, you're not very well. Shall I call somebody? Shall I get a glass of water?"

"No, no, no!" She threw herself toward him, her hand frantically clutching the newspaper. "I tell you, it's the man! I *know* him! He spoke to me in the garden!"

Parvis took the journal from her, directing his glasses to the portrait. "It can't be, Mrs. Boyne. It's Robert Elwell."

"Robert Elwell?" Her white stare seemed to travel into space. "Then it was Robert Elwell who came for him."

"Came for Boyne? The day he went away from here?" Parvis's voice dropped as hers rose. He bent over, laying a fraternal hand on her, as if to coax her gently back into her seat. "Why, Elwell was dead! Don't you remember?"

Mary sat with her eyes fixed on the picture, unconscious of what he was saying.

"Don't you remember Boyne's unfinished letter to me—the one you found on his desk that day? It was written just after he'd heard of Elwell's death." She noticed an odd shake in Parvis's unemotional voice. "Surely you remember!" he urged her.

Yes, she remembered: that was the profoundest horror of it. Elwell had died the day before her husband's disappearance; and this was Elwell's portrait; and it was the portrait of the man who had spoken to her in the garden. She lifted her head and looked slowly about the library. The library could have borne witness that it was also the portrait of the man who had come in that day to call Boyne from his unfinished letter. Through the misty surgings of her brain she heard the faint boom of half-forgotten words—words spoken by Alida Stair on the lawn at Pangbourne before Boyne and his wife had ever seen the house at Lyng, or had imagined that they might one day live there.

"This was the man who spoke to me," she repeated.

She looked again at Parvis. He was trying to conceal his disturbance under what he probably imagined to be an expression of indulgent commiseration; but the edges of his lips were blue. "He thinks me mad; but I'm not mad," she reflected; and suddenly there flashed upon her a way of justifying her strange affirmation.

She sat quiet, controlling the quiver of her lips, and waiting till she could trust her voice; then she said, looking straight at Parvis: "Will you answer me one question, please? When was it that Robert Elwell tried to kill himself?"

"When—when?" Parvis stammered.

"Yes; the date. Please try to remember."

She saw that he was growing still more afraid of her. "I have a reason," she insisted.

"Yes, yes. Only I can't remember. About two months before, I should say."

"I want the date," she repeated.

Parvis picked up the newspaper. "We might see here," he said, still humouring her. He ran his eyes down the page. "Here it is. Last October—the—"

She caught the words from him. "The 20th, wasn't it?" With a sharp look at her, he verified. "Yes, the 20th. Then you *did* know?"

"I know now." Her gaze continued to travel past him. "Sunday, the 20th—that was the day he came first."

Parvis's voice was almost inaudible. "Came *here* first?"

"Yes."

"You saw him twice, then?"

"Yes, twice." She just breathed it at him. "He came first on the 20th of October. I remember the date because it was the day we went up Meldon Steep for the first time." She felt a faint gasp of inward laughter at the thought that but for that she might have forgotten.

Parvis continued to scrutinise her, as if trying to intercept her gaze.

"We saw him from the roof," she went on. "He came down the lime-avenue toward the house. He was dressed just as he is in that picture. My husband saw him first. He was frightened, and ran down ahead of me; but there was no one there. He had vanished."

"Elwell had vanished?" Parvis faltered.

"Yes." Their two whispers seemed to grope for each other. "I couldn't think what had happened. I see now. He *tried* to come then; but he wasn't dead enough—he couldn't reach us. He had to wait for two months to die; and then he came back again—and Ned went with him."

She nodded at Parvis with the look of triumph of a child who has worked out a difficult puzzle. But suddenly she lifted her hands with a desperate gesture, pressing them to her temples.

"Oh, my God! I sent him to Ned—I told him where to go! I sent him to this room!" she screamed.

She felt the walls of books rush toward her, like inward falling ruins; and she heard Parvis, a long way off, through the ruins, crying to her, and struggling to get at her. But she was numb to his touch, she did not know what he was saying. Through the tumult she heard but one clear note, the voice of Alida Stair, speaking on the lawn at Pangbourne.

"You won't know till afterward," it said. "You won't know till long, long afterward."

THE TRACTATE MIDDOTH (1911)

M.R. James (1862–1936)

Montague Rhodes "Monty" James was one of the greatest and most influential writers of ghost stories in the twentieth century. An academic and a manuscripts expert at Cambridge University for much of his life, in 1893 James started a tradition of writing ghost stories to read to friends at Christmas. This story comes from his second collection of stories, *More Ghost Stories* (1911). His narratives are infused with his own interest in antiquarianism and often feature the motif of a found manuscript or other artefact which unleashes a ghost or demon onto the unsuspecting academic who studies it.

James was not only influential in the manner of his style; the very act of a scholar writing ghost stories proceeded to have a far-reaching influence, as friends and colleagues at Cambridge such as E.G. Swain, and the brothers E.F. and A.C. Benson, took to writing tales of their own.

'The Tractate Middoth' is set partially in Cambridge University Library, in its original location within the "Old Schools" (the present building was not constructed until the 1930s). It is possibly the most overtly bookish of all James's stories, and has the other distinction of being one of several stories in which his lifelong fear of spiders makes an appearance.

T OWARDS THE END OF AN AUTUMN AFTERNOON AN ELDERLY man with a thin face and grey Piccadilly weepers pushed open the swing door leading into the vestibule of a certain famous library, and addressing himself to an attendant, stated that he believed he was entitled to use the library, and inquired if he might take a book out. Yes, if he were on the list of those to whom that privilege was given. He produced his card—Mr. John Eldred—and, the register being consulted, a favourable answer was given. "Now, another point," said he. "It is a long time since I was here, and I do not know my way about your building; besides, it is near closing-time, and it is bad for me to hurry up and down stairs. I have here the title of the book I want: is there any one at liberty who could go and find it for me?" After a moment's thought the doorkeeper beckoned to a young man who was passing. "Mr. Garrett," he said, "have you a minute to assist this gentleman?" "With pleasure," was Mr. Garrett's answer. The slip with the title was handed to him. "I think I can put my hand on this; it happens to be in the class I inspected last quarter, but I'll just look it up in the catalogue to make sure. I suppose it is that particular edition that you require, sir?" "Yes, if you please; that, and no other," said Mr. Eldred; "I am exceedingly obliged to you." "Don't mention it, I beg, sir," said Mr. Garrett, and hurried off.

"I thought so," he said to himself, when his finger, travelling down the pages of the catalogue, stopped at a particular entry. "Talmud: Tractate Middoth, with the commentary of Nachmanides, Amsterdam, 1707. 11.3.34. Hebrew class, of course. Not a very difficult job this."

Mr. Eldred, accommodated with a chair in the vestibule, awaited anxiously the return of his messenger—and his disappointment at seeing an empty-handed Mr. Garrett running down the staircase was very evident. "I'm sorry to disappoint you, sir," said the young man, "but the book is out." "Oh dear!" said Mr. Eldred, "is that so? You are sure there can be no mistake?" "I don't think there is much chance of it, sir; but it's possible, if you like to wait a minute, that you might meet the very gentleman that's got it. He must be leaving the library soon, and I *think* I saw him take that particular book out of the shelf." "Indeed! You didn't recognise him, I suppose? Would it be one of the professors or one of the students?" "I don't think so: certainly not a professor. I should have known him; but the light isn't very good in that part of the library at this time of day, and I didn't see his face. I should have said he was a shortish old gentleman, perhaps a clergyman, in a cloak. If you could wait, I can easily find out whether he wants the book very particularly."

"No, no," said Mr. Eldred, "I won't—I can't wait now, thank you—no. I must be off. But I'll call again to-morrow if I may, and perhaps you could find out who has it."

"Certainly, sir, and I'll have the book ready for you if we—" but Mr. Eldred was already off, and hurrying more than one would have thought wholesome for him.

Garrett had a few moments to spare; and, thought he, "I'll go back to that case and see if I can find the old man. Most likely he could put off using the book for a few days. I dare say the other one doesn't want to keep it for long." So off with him to the Hebrew class. But when he got there it was unoccupied, and the volume marked 11.3.34 was in its place on the shelf. It was vexatious to Garrett's self-respect to have disappointed an inquirer with so little reason: and he would have liked, had it not been against library rules, to take the book down to the vestibule then and there, so that it might be ready for Mr. Eldred when he called. However, next morning he would be on the look-out for him, and he begged the doorkeeper to send and let him know when the moment came. As a matter of fact he was himself in the vestibule when Mr. Eldred arrived, very soon after the library opened, and when hardly anyone besides the staff were in the building.

"I'm very sorry," he said; "it's not often that I make such a stupid mistake, but I did feel sure that the old gentleman I saw took out that very book and kept it in his hand without opening it, just as people do, you know, sir, when they mean to take a book out of the library and not merely refer to it. But, however, I'll run up now at once and get it for you this time."

And here intervened a pause. Mr. Eldred paced the entry, read all the notices, consulted his watch, sat and gazed up the staircase, did all that a very impatient man could, until some twenty minutes had run out. At last he addressed himself to the doorkeeper and inquired if it was a very long way to that part of the library to which Mr. Garrett had gone.

"Well, I was thinking it was funny, sir: he's a quick man as a rule, but to be sure he might have been sent for by the libarian, but even so I think he'd have mentioned to him that you was waiting. I'll just speak him up on the toob and see." And to the tube he addressed himself. As he absorbed the reply to his question his face changed, and he made one or two supplementary inquiries which were shortly answered. Then he came forward to his counter and spoke in a lower tone. "I'm sorry to hear, sir, that something seems to have 'appened a little awkward. Mr. Garrett has been took poorly, it appears, and the libarian sent him 'ome in a cab the other way. Something of an attack, by what I can hear." "What, really? Do you mean that some one has injured him?" "No, sir, not violence 'ere, but, as I should judge, attacted with an attack, what you might term it, of illness. Not a strong constitootion, Mr. Garrett. But as to your book, sir, perhaps you might be able to find it for yourself. It's too bad you should be disappointed this way twice over—" "Er—well, but I'm so sorry that Mr. Garrett should have been taken ill in this way while he was obliging me. I think I must leave the book, and call and inquire after him. You can give me his address, I suppose." That was easily done: Mr. Garrett, it appeared, lodged in rooms not far from the station. "And, one other question. Did you happen to notice if an old gentleman, perhaps a clergyman, in a—yes—in a black cloak, left the library after I did yesterday. I think he may have been a—I think, that is, that he may be staying—or rather that I may have known him."

"Not in a black cloak, sir; no. There were only two gentlemen left later than what you done, sir, both of them youngish men. There was Mr. Carter took out a music-book and one of the prefessors with a couple o' novels. That's the lot, sir; and then I went off to me tea, and glad to get it. Thank you, sir, much obliged."

Mr. Eldred, still a prey to anxiety, betook himself in a cab to Mr. Garrett's address, but the young man was not yet in a condition to receive visitors. He was better, but his landlady considered that he must have had a severe shock. She thought most likely from what the doctor said that he would be able to see Mr. Eldred tomorrow. Mr. Eldred returned to his hotel at dusk and spent, I fear, but a dull evening.

On the next day he was able to see Mr. Garrett. When in health Mr. Garrett was a cheerful and pleasant-looking young man. Now he was a very white and shaky being, propped up in an armchair by the fire, and inclined to shiver and keep an eye on the door. If however there were visitors whom he was not prepared to welcome, Mr. Eldred was not among them. "It really is I who owe you an apology, and I was despairing of being able to pay it, for I didn't know your address. But I am very glad you have called. I do dislike and regret giving all this trouble, but you know I could not have foreseen this—this attack which I had."

"Of course not; but now, I am something of a doctor. You'll excuse my asking; you have had, I am sure, good advice. Was it a fall you had?"

"No. I did fall on the floor—but not from any height. It was, really, a shock."

"You mean something startled you. Was it anything you thought you saw?"

"Not much *thinking* in the case, I'm afraid. Yes, it was something I saw. You remember when you called the first time at the library?"

"Yes, of course. Well, now, let me beg you not to try to describe it—it will not be good for you to recall it, I'm sure."

"But indeed it would be a relief to me to tell any one like yourself: you might be able to explain it away. It was just when I was going into the class where your book is—"

"Indeed, Mr. Garrett, I insist; besides, my watch tells me I have but very little time left in which to get my things together and take the train. No—not another word—it would be more distressing to you than you imagine, perhaps. Now there is just one thing I want to say. I feel that I am really indirectly responsible for this illness of yours, and I think I ought to defray the expense which it has—eh?"

But this offer was quite distinctly declined. Mr. Eldred, not pressing it, left almost at once: not however, before Mr. Garrett had insisted upon his taking a note of the class mark of the Tractate

Middoth, which, as he said, Mr. Eldred could at leisure get for himself. But Mr. Eldred did not reappear at the library.

William Garrett had another visitor that day in the person of a contemporary and colleague from the library, one George Earle. Earle had been one of those who found Garrett lying insensible on the floor just inside the "class" or cubicle (opening upon the central alley of a spacious gallery) in which the Hebrew books were placed, and Earle had naturally been very anxious about his friend's condition. So as soon as library hours were over he appeared at the lodgings. "Well," he said (after other conversation), "I've no notion what it was that put you wrong, but I've got the idea that there's something wrong in the atmosphere of the library. I know this, that just before we found you I was coming along the gallery with Davis, and I said to him, 'Did ever you know such a musty smell anywhere as there is about here? It can't be wholesome.' Well now, if one goes on living a long time with a smell of that kind (I tell you it was worse than I ever knew it) it must get into the system and break out some time, don't you think?"

Garrett shook his head. "That's all very well about the smell— but it isn't always there, though I've noticed it the last day or two—a sort of unnaturally strong smell of dust. But no—that's not what did for me. It was something I *saw.* And I want to tell you about it. I went into that Hebrew class to get a book for a man that was inquiring for it down below. Now that same book I'd made a mistake about the day before. I'd been for it, for the same man, and made sure that I saw an old parson in a cloak taking it out. I told my man it was out: off he went, to call again next day. I went back to see if I could get it out of the parson: no parson there, and the book on the shelf. Well, yesterday, as I say, I went again. This time, if you please—ten o'clock in the morning, remember, and as much light as ever you get in those classes, and there was my parson again, back to me, looking at the books on the shelf I wanted. His hat was on the table, and he had a bald head. I waited a second or two looking at him rather particularly. I tell you, he had a very nasty bald head. It looked to me dry, and it looked dusty, and the streaks of hair across it were much less like hair than like cobwebs. Well, I made a bit of a noise on purpose, coughed and moved my feet. He turned round and let me see his face—which I hadn't seen before. I tell you again, I'm not mistaken. Though, for one reason or another I didn't take in the lower part of his face, I did see the upper part; and it was perfectly dry, and the eyes were very deep-sunk; and over them, from the eyebrows to the cheek-bone there were *cobwebs*—thick. Now that closed me up, as they say, and I can't tell you anything more."

What explanations were furnished by Earle of this phenomenon it does not very much concern us to inquire; at all events they did not convince Garrett that he had not seen what he had seen.

Before William Garrett returned to work at the library, the librarian insisted upon his taking a week's rest and change of air. Within a few days' time, therefore, he was at the station with his bag, looking for a desirable smoking compartment in which to travel to Burnstow-on-Sea, which he had not previously visited. One compartment and one only seemed to be suitable. But, just as he approached it, he saw, standing in front of the door, a figure so like one bound up with recent unpleasant associations that, with a sickening qualm, and hardly knowing what he did, he tore open the door of the next compartment and pulled himself into it as quickly as if Death were at his heels. The train moved off, and he must have turned quite faint, for he was next conscious of a smelling-bottle being put to his nose. His physician was a nice-looking old lady, who, with her daughter, was the only passenger in the carriage.

But for this incident it is not very likely that he would have made any overtures to his fellow-travellers. As it was, thanks and inquiries and general conversation supervened inevitably: and Garrett found himself provided before the journey's end not only with a physician, but with a landlady: for Mrs. Simpson had apartments to let at Burnstow, which seemed in all ways suitable. The place was empty at that season, so that Garrett was thrown a good deal into the society of the mother and daughter. He found them very acceptable company. On the third evening of his stay he was on such terms with them as to be asked to spend the evening in their private sitting-room.

During their talk it transpired that Garrett's work lay in a library. "Ah, libraries are fine places," said Mrs. Simpson, putting down her work with a sigh; "but for all that, books have played me a sad turn, or rather *a* book has."

"Well, books give me my living, Mrs. Simpson, and I should be sorry to say a word against them: I don't like to hear that they have been bad for you."

"Perhaps Mr. Garrett could help us to solve our puzzle, Mother," said Miss Simpson.

"I don't want to set Mr. Garrett off on a hunt that might waste a lifetime, my dear, nor yet to trouble him with our private affairs."

"But if you think it in the least likely that I could be of use, I do beg you to tell me what the puzzle is, Mrs. Simpson. If it is finding out anything about a book, you see, I am in rather a good position to do it."

"Yes, I do see that, but the worst of it is that we don't know the name of the book."

"Nor what it is about?"

"No, nor that either."

"Except that we don't think it's in English, Mother—and that is not much of a clue."

"Well, Mr. Garrett," said Mrs. Simpson, who had not yet resumed her work, and was looking at the fire thoughtfully, "I shall tell you the story. You will please keep it to yourself, if you don't mind? Thank you. Now it is just this. I had an old uncle, a Dr. Rant. Perhaps you may have heard of him. Not that he was a distinguished man, but from the odd way he chose to be buried."

"I rather think I have seen the name in some guide-book."

"That would be it," said Miss Simpson. "He left directions—horrid old man!—that he was to be put, sitting at a table in his ordinary clothes, in a brick room that he'd had made underground in a field near his house. Of course the country people say he's been seen about there in his old black cloak."

"Well, dear, I don't know much about such things," Mrs. Simpson went on, "but anyhow he is dead, these twenty years and more. He was a clergyman, though I'm sure I can't imagine how he got to be one: but he did no duty for the last part of his life, which I think was a good thing; and he lived on his own property: a very nice estate not a great way from here. He had no wife or family; only one niece, who was myself, and one nephew, and he had no particular liking for either of us—nor for any one else, as far as that goes. If anything, he liked my cousin better than he did me—for John was much more like him in his temper, and, I'm afraid I must say, his very mean sharp ways. It might have been different if I had not married; but I did, and that he very much resented. Very well:

here he was with this estate and a good deal of money, as it turned out, of which he had the absolute disposal, and it was understood that we—my cousin and I—would share it equally at his death. In a certain winter, over twenty years back, as I said, he was taken ill, and I was sent for to nurse him. My husband was alive then, but the old man would not hear of *his* coming. As I drove up to the house I saw my cousin John driving away from it in an open fly and looking, I noticed, in very good spirits. I went up and did what I could for my uncle, but I was very soon sure that this would be his last illness; and he was convinced of it too. During the day before he died he got me to sit by him all the time, and I could see there was something, and probably something unpleasant, that he was saving up to tell me, and putting it off as long as he felt he could afford the strength—I'm afraid purposely in order to keep me on the stretch. But, at last, out it came. 'Mary,' he said,—'Mary, I've made my will in John's favour; he has everything, Mary.' Well, of course that came as a bitter shock to me, for we—my husband and I—were not rich people, and if he could have managed to live a little easier than he was obliged to do, I felt it might be the prolonging of his life. But I said little or nothing to my uncle, except that he had a right to do what he pleased: partly because I could not think of anything to say, and partly because I was sure there was more to come: and so there was. 'But Mary,' he said, 'I'm not very fond of John, and I've made another will in *your* favour. *You* can have everything. Only you've got to find the will, you see: and I don't mean to tell you where it is.' Then he chuckled to himself, and I waited, for again I was sure he hadn't finished. 'That's a good girl,' he said after a time,—'you wait, and I'll tell you as much as I told John. But just let me remind you, you can't go into court with what I'm saying to you, for *you* won't be able to produce any collateral evidence beyond your own

word, and John's a man that can do a little hard swearing if necessary. Very well then, that's understood. Now, I had the fancy that I
wouldn't write this will quite in the common way, so I wrote it in
a book, Mary, a printed book. And there's several thousand books
in this house. But there! you needn't trouble yourself with them,
for it isn't one of them. It's in safe keeping elsewhere: in a place
where John can go and find it any day, if he only knew, and you
can't. A good will it is: properly signed and witnessed, but I don't
think you'll find the witnesses in a hurry.'

"Still I said nothing: if I had moved at all I must have taken hold
of the old wretch and shaken him. He lay there laughing to himself,
and at last he said—

"'Well, well, you've taken it very quietly, and as I want to start
you both on equal terms, and John has a bit of a purchase in being
able to go where the book is, I'll tell you just two other things
which I didn't tell him. The will's in English, but you won't know
that if ever you see it. That's one thing, and another is that when
I'm gone you'll find an envelope in my desk directed to you, and
inside it something that would help you to find it, if only you have
the wits to use it.'

"In a few hours from that he was gone, and though I made an
appeal to John Eldred about it—"

"John Eldred? I beg your pardon, Mrs. Simpson—I think I've
seen a Mr. John Eldred. What is he like to look at?"

"It must be ten years since I saw him: he would be a thin
elderly man now, and unless he has shaved them off, he has that
sort of whiskers which people used to call Dundreary or Piccadilly
something."

"—weepers. Yes, that *is* the man."

"Where did you come across him, Mr. Garrett?"

"I don't know if I could tell you," said Garrett mendaciously, "in some public place. But you hadn't finished."

"Really I had nothing much to add, only that John Eldred, of course, paid no attention whatever to my letters, and has enjoyed the estate ever since, while my daughter and I have had to take to the lodging-house business here, which I must say has not turned out by any means so unpleasant as I feared it might."

"But about the envelope."

"To be sure! Why the puzzle turns on that. Give Mr. Garrett the paper out of my desk."

It was a small slip, with nothing whatever on it but five numerals, not divided or punctuated in any way: 11334.

Mr. Garrett pondered, but there was a light in his eye. Suddenly he "made a face," and then asked, "Do you suppose that Mr. Eldred can have any more clue than you have to the title of the book?"

"I have sometimes thought he must," said Mrs. Simpson, "and in this way: that my uncle must have made the will not very long before he died (that, I think, he said himself), and got rid of the book immediately afterwards. But all his books were very carefully catalogued: and John has the catalogue: and John was most particular that no books whatever should be sold out of the house. And I'm told that he is always journeying about to booksellers and libraries; so I fancy that he must have found out just which books are missing from my uncle's library of those which are entered in the catalogue, and must be hunting for them."

"Just so, just so," said Mr. Garrett, and relapsed into thought.

No later than next day he received a letter which, as he told Mrs. Simpson with great regret, made it absolutely necessary for him to cut short his stay at Burnstow.

Sorry as he was to leave them (and they were at least as sorry to part with him), he had begun to feel that a crisis, all-important to Mrs. (and shall we add, Miss?) Simpson, was very possibly supervening.

In the train Garrett was uneasy and excited. He racked his brains to think whether the press mark of the book which Mr. Eldred had been inquiring after was one in any way corresponding to the numbers on Mrs. Simpson's little bit of paper. But he found to his dismay that the shock of the previous week had really so upset him that he could neither remember any vestige of the title or nature of the book, or even of the locality to which he had gone to seek it. And yet all other parts of library topography and work were clear as ever in his mind.

And another thing—he stamped with annoyance as he thought of it—he had at first hesitated, and then had forgotten, to ask Mrs. Simpson for the name of the place where Eldred lived. That, however, he could write about.

At least he had his due in the figures on the paper. If they referred to a press mark in his library, they were only susceptible of a limited number of interpretations. They might be divided into 1.13.34, 11.33.4, or 11.3.34. He could try all these in the space of a few minutes, and if any one were missing he had every means of tracing it. He got very quickly to work, though a few minutes had to be spent in explaining his early return to his landlady and his colleagues. 1.13.34 was in place and contained no extraneous writing. As he drew near to Class 11 in the same gallery, its association struck him like a chill. But he *must* go on. After a cursory glance at 11.33.4 (which first confronted him, and was a perfectly new book) he ran his eye along the line of quartos which fills 11.3. The gap he feared was there: 34

was out. A moment was spent in making sure that it had not been misplaced, and then he was off to the vestibule.

"Has 11.3.34 gone out? Do you recollect noticing that number?"

"Notice the number? What do you take me for, Mr. Garrett? There, take and look over the tickets for yourself, if you've got a free day before you."

"Well then, has a Mr. Eldred called again—the old gentleman who came the day I was taken ill. Come! you'd remember him."

"What do you suppose? Of course I recollect of him: no, he haven't been in again, not since you went off for your 'oliday. And yet I seem to—there now. Roberts 'll know. Roberts, do you recollect of the name of Heldred?"

"Not arf," said Roberts. "You mean the man that sent a bob over the price for the parcel, and I wish they all did."

"Do you mean to say you've been sending books to Mr. Eldred? Come, do speak up! Have you?"

"Well now, Mr. Garrett, if a gentleman sends the ticket ail wrote correct and the secketry says this book may go and the box ready addressed sent with the note, and a sum of money sufficient to deefray the railway charges, what would be *your* action in the matter, Mr. Garrett, if I may take the liberty to ask such a question? Would you or would you not have taken the trouble to oblige, or would you have chucked the 'ole thing under the counter and—"

"You were perfectly right, of course, Hodgson—perfectly right: only, would you kindly oblige me by showing me the ticket Mr. Eldred sent, and letting me know his address?"

"To be sure, Mr. Garrett, so long as I'm not 'ectored about and informed that I don't know my duty, I'm willing to oblige in every way feasible to my power. There is the ticket on the file. J. Eldred,

11.3.34. Title of work: T—a—i—m—well, there, you can make what you like of it—not a novel, I should 'azard the guess. And here is Mr. Heldred's note applying for the book in question, which I see he terms it a track."

"Thanks, thanks: but the address? There's none on the note."

"Ah, indeed; well, now... stay now, Mr. Garrett, I 'ave it. Why, that note come inside of the parcel, which was directed very thoughtful to save all trouble, ready to be sent back with the book inside; and if I *have* made any mistake in this 'ole transaction, it lays just in the one point that I neglected to enter the address in my little book here what I keep. Not but what I daresay there was good reasons for me not entering of it: but there, I haven't the time, neither have you, I dare say, to go into 'em just now. And—no, Mr. Garrett, I do *not* carry it in my 'ed, else what would be the use of me keeping this little book here—just a ordinary common notebook, you see, which I make a practice of entering all such names and addresses in it as I see fit to do?"

"Admirable arrangement, to be sure—but—all right, thank you. When did the parcel go off?"

"Half-past ten, this morning."

"Oh, good; and it's just one now."

Garrett went upstairs in deep thought. How was he to get the address? A telegram to Mrs. Simpson: he might miss a train by waiting for the answer. Yes, there was one other way. She had said that Eldred lived on his uncle's estate. If this were so, he might find that place entered in the donation-book. That he could run through quickly, now that he knew the title of the book. The register was soon before him, and, knowing that the old man had died more than twenty years ago, he gave him a good margin, and turned back to 1870. There was but one entry possible. "1875, August 14th.

Talmud: Tractatus Middoth cum comm. R. Nachmanidoe. Amstelod.
1707. Given by J. Rant, D. D., of Bretfield Manor."

A gazetteer showed Bretfield to be three miles from a small station on the main line. Now to ask the doorkeeper whether he recollected if the name on the parcel had been anything like Bretfield.

"No, nothing like. It was, now you mention it, Mr. Garrett,
either Bredfield or Britfield, but nothing like that other name what
you coated."

So far well. Next, a time-table. A train could be got in twenty
minutes—taking two hours over the journey. The only chance, but
one not to be missed; and the train was taken.

If he had been fidgety on the journey up, he was almost distracted on the journey down. If he found Eldred, what could he
say? That it had been discovered that the book was a rarity and must
be recalled? An obvious untruth. Or that it was believed to contain
important manuscript notes? Eldred would of course show him the
book, from which the leaf would already have been removed. He
might, perhaps, find traces of the removal—a torn edge of a fly-leaf
probably—and who could disprove, what Eldred was certain to say,
that he too had noticed and regretted the mutilation? Altogether the
chase seemed very hopeless. The one chance was this. The book
had left the library at 10.30: it might not have been put into the
first possible train, at 11.20. Granted that, then he might be lucky
enough to arrive simultaneously with it and patch up some story
which would induce Eldred to give it up.

It was drawing towards evening when he got out upon the
platform of his station, and, like most country stations, this one
seemed unnaturally quiet. He waited about till the one or two pas-
sengers who got out with him had drifted off, and then inquired of
the stationmaster whether Mr. Eldred was in the neighbourhood.

"Yes, and pretty near too, I believe. I fancy he means calling here for a parcel he expects. Called for it once to-day already, didn't he, Bob?" (to the porter).

"Yes sir, he did; and appeared to think it was all along of me that it didn't come by the two o'clock. Anyhow, I've got it for him now," and the porter flourished a square parcel, which a glance assured Garrett contained all that was of any importance to him at that particular moment.

"Bretfield, sir? Yes—three miles just about. Short cut across these three fields brings it down by half a mile. There: there's Mr. Eldred's trap."

A dog-cart drove up with two men in it, of whom Garrett, gazing back as he crossed the little station yard, easily recognised one. The fact that Eldred was driving was slightly in his favour—for most likely he would not open the parcel in the presence of his servant. On the other hand, he would get home quickly, and unless Garrett were there within a very few minutes of his arrival, all would be over. He must hurry; and that he did. His short cut took him along one side of a triangle, while the cart had two sides to traverse; and it was delayed a little at the station, so that Garrett was in the third of the three fields when he heard the wheels fairly near. He had made the best progress possible, but the pace at which the cart was coming made him despair. At this rate it *must* reach home ten minutes before him, and ten minutes would more than suffice for the fulfilment of Mr. Eldred's project.

It was just at this time that the luck fairly turned. The evening was still, and sounds came clearly. Seldom has any sound given greater relief than that which he now heard: that of the cart pulling up. A few words were exchanged, and it drove on. Garrett, halting in the utmost anxiety, was able to see as it drove past the stile (near which he now stood), that it contained only the servant and not Eldred; further, he made out that Eldred was following on foot. From behind the tall hedge by the stile leading into the road he watched the thin wiry figure pass quickly by with the parcel beneath its arm, and feeling in its pockets. Just as he passed the stile something fell out of a pocket upon the grass, but with so little sound that Eldred was not conscious of it. In a moment more it was safe for Garrett to cross the stile into the road and pick up—a box of matches. Eldred went on, and, as he went, his arms made hasty movements, difficult to interpret in the shadow of the trees that overhung the road. But, as Garrett followed cautiously, he found at various points the key to them—a piece of string, and then the wrapper of the parcel—meant to be thrown *over* the hedge, but sticking in it.

Now Eldred was walking slower, and it could just be made out that he had opened the book and was turning over the leaves. He stopped, evidently troubled by the failing light. Garrett slipped into a gate-opening, but still watched. Eldred, hastily looking around, sat down on a felled tree-trunk by the roadside and held the open book up close to his eyes. Suddenly he laid it, still open, on his knee, and felt in all his pockets: clearly in vain, and clearly to his annoyance. "You would be glad of your matches now," thought Garrett. Then he took hold of a leaf, and was carefully tearing it out, when two things happened. First, something black seemed to drop upon the white leaf and run down it, and then as Eldred started and was turning to look behind him, a little dark form appeared to rise out of the shadow behind the tree-trunk and from it two arms enclosing a mass of blackness came before Eldred's face and covered his head and neck. His legs and arms were wildly flourished, but no sound came. Then, there was no more movement. Eldred was alone. He had fallen back into the grass behind the tree-trunk. The book was cast into the roadway. Garrett, his anger and suspicion gone for the moment at the sight of this horrid struggle, rushed up with loud cries of "Help!" and so too, to his enormous relief, did a labourer who had just emerged from a field opposite. Together they bent over and supported Eldred, but to no purpose. The conclusion that he was dead was inevitable. "Poor gentleman!" said Garrett to the labourer, when they had laid him down, "what happened to him, do you think?" "I wasn't two hundred yards away," said the man, "when I see Squire Eldred setting reading in his book, and to my thinking he was took with one of these fits—face seemed to go all over black." "Just so," said Garrett. "You didn't see any one near him. It couldn't have been an assault?" "Not possible—no one couldn't have got away without you or me seeing them." "So I thought. Well, we must get some help, and the doctor and the policeman; and perhaps I had better give them this book."

It was obviously a case for an inquest, and obvious also that Garrett must stay at Bretfield and give his evidence. The medical inspection showed that, though some black dust was found on the face and in the mouth of the deceased, the cause of death was a shock to a weak heart, and not asphyxiation. The fateful book was produced, a respectable quarto printed wholly in Hebrew, and not of an aspect likely to excite even the most sensitive.

"You say, Mr. Garrett, that the deceased gentleman appeared at the moment before his attack to be tearing a leaf out of this book?"

"Yes; I think one of the fly-leaves."

"There is here a fly-leaf partially torn through. It has Hebrew writing on it. Will you kindly inspect it?"

"There are three names in English, sir, also, and a date. But I am sorry to say I cannot read Hebrew writing."

"Thank you. The names have the appearance of being signatures. They are John Rant, Walter Gibson, and James Frost, and the date is 20 July, 1875. Does any one here know any of these names?"

The Rector, who was present, volunteered a statement that the uncle of the deceased, from whom he inherited, had been named Rant.

The book being handed to him, he shook a puzzled head. "This is not like any Hebrew I ever learnt."

"You are sure that it is Hebrew?"

"What? Yes—I suppose No—my dear sir, you are perfectly right—that is, your suggestion is exactly to the point. Of course—it is not Hebrew at all. It is English, and it is a will."

It did not take many minutes to show that here was indeed a will of Dr. John Rant, bequeathing the whole of the property lately held by John Eldred to Mrs. Mary Simpson. Clearly the discovery of such a document would amply justify Mr. Eldred's agitation. As to the partial tearing of the leaf, the coroner pointed out that no useful purpose could be attained by speculations whose correctness it would never be possible to establish.

The Tractate Middoth was naturally taken in charge by the coroner for further investigation, and Mr. Garrett explained privately to him the history of it, and the position of events so far as he knew or guessed them.

He returned to his work next day, and on his walk to the station passed the scene of Mr. Eldred's catastrophe. He could hardly leave it without another look, though the recollection of what he had seen there made him shiver, even on that bright morning. He walked round, with some misgivings, behind the felled tree. Something dark that still lay there made him start back for a moment: but it hardly stirred. Looking closer, he saw that it was a thick black mass of cobwebs; and, as he stirred it gingerly with his stick, several large spiders ran out of it into the grass.

There is no great difficulty in imagining the steps by which William Garrett, from being an assistant in a great library, attained to his present position of prospective owner of Bretfield Manor, now in the occupation of his mother-in-law, Mrs. Mary Simpson.

BONE TO HIS BONE (1912)

E.G. Swain (1861–1938)

Edmund Gill Swain was a close friend of M.R. James, attending many of James's Christmas ghost story readings and also working together to stage amateur theatricals. He was a contemporary of James at Cambridge, and was made the chaplain of King's College while James was the Dean there. The two remained good friends after 1905, when Swain left Cambridge, having been appointed vicar of Stanground, a village near Peterborough. In 1912, Swain published *The Stoneground Ghost Tales*, a series of connected ghost stories inspired by his new parish, and featuring a fictionalised version of himself: Mr. Batchel, the rector of Stoneground.

Swain shared James's antiquarian interests, and had an enthusiasm for archaeology, which is evident in this story. He did not hold absolutely to James's guidance for a successful ghost story, though. In the preface to his 1911 collection, *More Ghost Stories*, James wrote, "The ghost should be malevolent or odious: amiable and helpful apparitions are all very well in fairy tales or in local legends, but I have no use for them in a fictitious ghost story." Although admittedly 'Bone to his Bone' is not as frightening as the best of James, the subtle understanding between ghost and vicar makes this story special.

W ILLIAM WHITEHEAD, FELLOW OF EMMANUEL COLLEGE, in the University of Cambridge, became Vicar of Stoneground in the year 1731. The annals of his incumbency were doubtless short and simple: they have not survived. In his day were no newspapers to collect gossip, no parish magazines to record the simple events of parochial life. One event, however, of greater moment then than now, is recorded in two places. Vicar Whitehead failed in health after twenty-three years of work, and journeyed to Bath in what his monument calls "the vain hope of being restored". The duration of his visit is unknown; it is reasonable to suppose that he made his journey in the summer, it is certain that by the month of November his physician told him to lay aside all hope of recovery.

Then it was that the thoughts of the patient turned to the comfortable straggling vicarage he had left at Stoneground, in which he had hoped to end his days. He prayed that his successor might be as happy there as he had been himself. Setting his affairs in order, as became one who had but a short time to live, he executed a will, bequeathing to the Vicars of Stoneground, for ever, the close of ground he had recently purchased because it lay next the vicarage garden. And by a codicil, he added to the bequest his library of books. Within a few days, William Whitehead was gathered to his fathers.

A mural tablet in the north aisle of the church, records, in Latin, his services and his bequests, his two marriages, and his fruitless journey to Bath. The house he loved, but never again saw, was taken down forty years later, and re-built by Vicar James Devie.

The garden, with Vicar Whitehead's "close of ground" and other adjacent lands, was opened out and planted, somewhat before 1850, by Vicar Robert Towerson. The aspect of everything has changed. But in a convenient chamber on the first floor of the present vicarage the library of Vicar Whitehead stands very much as he used it and loved it, and as he bequeathed it to his successors "for ever".

The books there are arranged as he arranged and ticketed them. Little slips of paper, sometimes bearing interesting fragments of writing, still mark his places. His marginal comments still give life to pages from which all other interest has faded, and he would have but a dull imagination who could sit in the chamber amidst these books without ever being carried back 180 years into the past, to the time when the newest of them left the printer's hands.

Of those into whose possession the books have come, some have doubtless loved them more, and some less; some, perhaps, have left them severely alone. But neither those who loved them, nor those who loved them not, have lost them, and they passed, some century and a half after William Whitehead's death, into the hands of Mr. Batchel, who loved them as a father loves his children. He lived alone, and had few domestic cares to distract his mind. He was able, therefore, to enjoy to the full what Vicar Whitehead had enjoyed so long before him. During many a long summer evening would he sit poring over long-forgotten books; and since the chamber, otherwise called the library, faced the south, he could also spend sunny winter mornings there without discomfort. Writing at a small table, or reading as he stood at a tall desk, he would browse amongst the books like an ox in a pleasant pasture.

There were other times also, at which Mr. Batchel would use the books. Not being a sound sleeper (for book-loving men seldom are), he elected to use as a bedroom one of the two chambers which

opened at either side into the library. The arrangement enabled
him to beguile many a sleepless hour amongst the books, and in
view of these nocturnal visits he kept a candle standing in a sconce
above the desk, and matches always ready to his hand.

There was one disadvantage in this close proximity of his bed
to the library. Owing, apparrently, to some defect in the fittings
of the room, which, having no mechanical tastes, Mr. Batchel had
never investigated, there could be heard, in the stillness of the
night, exactly such sounds as might arise from a person moving
about amongst the books. Visitors using the other adjacent room
would often remark at breakfast, that they had heard their host in
the library at one or two o'clock in the morning, when, in fact, he
had not left his bed. Invariably Mr. Batchel allowed them to suppose that he had been where they thought him. He disliked idle
controversy, and was unwilling to afford an opening for supernatural
talk. Knowing well enough the sounds by which his guests had been
deceived, he wanted no other explanation of them than his own,
though it was of too vague a character to count as an explanation.
He conjectured that the window-sashes, or the doors, or "something", were defective, and was too phlegmatic and too unpractical
to make any investigation. The matter gave him no concern.

Persons whose sleep is uncertain are apt to have their worst
nights when they would like their best. The consciousness of a
special need for rest seems to bring enough mental disturbance to
forbid it. So on Christmas Eve, in the year 1907, Mr. Batchel, who
would have liked to sleep well, in view of the labours of Christmas
Day, lay hopelessly wide awake. He exhausted all the known devices
for courting sleep, and, at the end, found himself wider awake than
ever. A brilliant moon shone into his room, for he hated window-
blinds. There was a light wind blowing, and the sounds in the library

were more than usually suggestive of a person moving about. He almost determined to have the sashes "seen to", although he could seldom be induced to have anything "seen to". He disliked changes, even for the better, and would submit to great inconvenience rather than have things altered with which he had become familiar.

As he revolved these matters in his mind, he heard the clocks strike the hour of midnight, and having now lost all hope of falling asleep, he rose from his bed, got into a large dressing gown which hung in readiness for such occasions, and passed into the library, with the intention of reading himself sleepy, if he could.

The moon, by this time, had passed out of the south, and the library seemed all the darker by contrast with the moonlit chamber he had left. He could see nothing but two blue-grey rectangles formed by the windows against the sky, the furniture of the room being altogether invisible. Groping along to where the table stood, Mr. Batchel felt over its surface for the matches which usually lay there; he found, however, that the table was cleared of everything. He raised his right hand, therefore, in order to feel his way to a shelf where the matches were sometimes mislaid, and at that moment, whilst his hand was in mid-air, the matchbox was gently put into it!

Such an incident could hardly fail to disturb even a phlegmatic person, and Mr. Batchel cried "Who's this?" somewhat nervously. There was no answer. He struck a match, looked hastily round the room, and found it empty, as usual. There was everything, that is to say, that he was accustomed to see, but no other person than himself.

It is not quite accurate, however, to say that everything was in its usual state. Upon the tall desk lay a quarto volume that he had certainly not placed there. It was his quite invariable practice to replace his books upon the shelves after using them, and what we may call his library habits were precise and methodical. A book out of place like this, was not only an offence against good order, but a sign that his privacy had been intruded upon. With some surprise, therefore, he lit the candle standing ready in the sconce, and proceeded to examine the book, not sorry, in the disturbed condition in which he was, to have an occupation found for him.

The book proved to be one with which he was unfamiliar, and this made it certain that some other hand than his had removed it from its place. Its title was *The Compleat Gard'ner* of M. de la Quintinye made English by John Evelyn Esquire. It was not a work in which Mr. Batchel felt any great interest. It consisted of divers reflections on various parts of husbandry, doubtless entertaining enough, but too deliberate and discursive for practical purposes. He had certainly never used the book, and growing restless now in mind, said to himself that some boy having the freedom of the house, had taken it down from its place in the hope of finding pictures.

But even whilst he made this explanation he felt its weakness. To begin with, the desk was too high for a boy. The improbability that any boy would place a book there was equalled by the improbability that he would leave it there. To discover its uninviting character would be the work only of a moment, and no boy would have brought it so far from its shelf.

Mr. Batchel had, however, come to read, and habit was too strong with him to be wholly set aside. Leaving *The Compleat Gard'ner* on the desk, he turned round to the shelves to find some more congenial reading.

Hardly had he done this when he was startled by a sharp rap upon the desk behind him, followed by a rustling of paper. He turned quickly about and saw the quarto lying open. In obedience to the instinct of the moment, he at once sought a natural cause for what he saw. Only a wind, and that of the strongest, could have opened the book, and laid back its heavy cover; and though he accepted, for a brief moment, that explanation, he was too candid to retain it longer. The wind out of doors was very light. The window sash was closed and latched, and, to decide the matter finally, the book had its back, and not its edges, turned towards the only quarter from which a wind could strike.

Mr. Batchel approached the desk again and stood over the book. With increasing perturbation of mind (for he still thought of the matchbox) he looked upon the open page. Without much reason beyond that he felt constrained to do something, he read the words of the half completed sentence at the turn of the page—

"at dead of night he left the house and passed into the solitude of the garden."

But he read no more, nor did he give himself the trouble of discovering whose midnight wandering was being described, although the habit was singularly like one of his own. He was in no condition for reading, and turning his back upon the volume he slowly paced the length of the chamber, "wondering at that which had come to pass".

He reached the opposite end of the chamber and was in the act of turning, when again he heard the rustling of paper, and by the time he had faced round, saw the leaves of the book again turning over. In a moment the volume lay at rest, open in another place, and there was no further movement as he approached it. To make sure that he had not been deceived, he read again the words as they entered the page. The author was following a not uncommon practice of the time, and throwing common speech into forms suggested by Holy Writ: "So dig," it said, "that ye may obtain."

This passage, which to Mr. Batchel seemed reprehensible in its levity, excited at once his interest and his disapproval. He was prepared to read more, but this time was not allowed. Before his eye could pass beyond the passage already cited, the leaves of the book slowly turned again, and presented but a termination of five words and a colophon.

The words were, "to the North, an Ilex". These three passages, in which he saw no meaning and no connection, began to entangle themselves together in Mr. Batchel's mind. He found himself repeating them in different orders, now beginning with one, and now with another. Any further attempt at reading he felt to be impossible, and he was in no mind for any more experiences of the unaccountable. Sleep was, of course, further from him than ever, if that were conceivable. What he did, therefore, was to blow out the candle, to return to his moonlit bedroom, and put on more clothing, and then to pass downstairs with the object of going out of doors.

It was not unusual with Mr. Batchel to walk about his garden at night-time. This form of exercise had often, after a wakeful hour, sent him back to his bed refreshed and ready for sleep. The convenient access to the garden at such times lay through his study, whose French windows opened on to a short flight of steps, and upon these he now paused for a moment to admire the snow-like appearance of the lawns, bathed as they were in the moonlight. As he paused, he heard the city clocks strike the half-hour after midnight, and he could not forbear repeating aloud—

"At dead of night he left the house, and passed into the solitude of the garden."

It was solitary enough. At intervals the screech of an owl, and now and then the noise of a train, seemed to emphasise the solitude by drawing attention to it and then leaving it in possession of the night. Mr. Batchel found himself wondering and conjecturing what Vicar Whitehead, who had acquired the close of land to secure quiet and privacy for a garden, would have thought of the railways to the west and north. He turned his face northwards, whence a whistle had just sounded, and saw a tree beautifully outlined against the sky. His breath caught at the sight. Not because the tree was unfamiliar. Mr. Batchel knew all his trees. But what he had seen was "to the north, an Ilex".

Mr. Batchel knew not what to make of it all. He had walked into the garden hundreds of times and as often seen the Ilex, but the words out of the *Compleat Gard'ner* seemed to be pursuing him in a way that made him almost afraid. His temperament, however, as has been said already, was phlegmatic. It was commonly said, and Mr. Batchel approved the verdict, whilst he condemned its inexactness, that "his nerves were made of fiddle-string", so he braced himself afresh and set upon his walk round the silent garden, which he was accustomed to begin in a northerly direction, and was now too proud to change. He usually passed the Ilex at the beginning of his perambulation, and so would pass it now.

He did not pass it. A small discovery, as he reached it, annoyed and disturbed him. His gardener, as careful and punctilious as himself, never failed to house all his tools at the end of a day's work. Yet there, under the Ilex, standing upright in moonlight brilliant enough to cast a shadow of it, was a spade.

Mr. Batchel's second thought was one of relief. After his extraordinary experiences in the library (he hardly knew now whether they had been real or not) something quite commonplace would act sedatively, and he determined to carry the spade to the tool-house.

The soil was quite dry, and the surface even a little frozen, so Mr. Batchel left the path, walked up to the spade, and would have drawn it towards him. But it was as if he had made the attempt upon the trunk of the Ilex itself. The spade would not be moved. Then, first with one hand, and then with both, he tried to raise it, and still it stood firm. Mr. Batchel, of course, attributed this to the frost, slight as it was. Wondering at the spade's being there, and annoyed at its being frozen, he was about to leave it and continue his walk, when the remaining words of the *Compleat Gard'ner* seemed rather to utter themselves, than to await his will—

"So dig, that ye may obtain."

Mr. Batchel's power of independent action now deserted him. He took the spade, which no longer resisted, and began to dig. "Five spadefuls and no more," he said aloud. "This is all foolishness."

Four spadefuls of earth he then raised and spread out before him in the moonlight. There was nothing unusual to be seen. Nor did Mr. Batchel decide what he would look for, whether coins, jewels, documents in canisters, or weapons. In point of fact, he dug against what he deemed his better judgment, and expected nothing. He spread before him the fifth and last spadeful of earth, not quite without result, but with no result that was at all sensational. The earth contained a bone. Mr. Batchel's knowledge of anatomy was sufficient to show him that it was a human bone. He identified it, even by moonlight, as the *radius,* a bone of the forearm, as he removed the earth from it, with his thumb.

Such a discovery might be thought worthy of more than the very ordinary interest Mr. Batchel showed. As a matter of fact, the presence of a human bone was easily to be accounted for. Recent excavations within the church had caused the upturning of numberless bones, which had been collected and reverently buried. But an earth-stained bone is also easily overlooked, and this *radius* had obviously found its way into the garden with some of the earth brought out of the church.

Mr. Batchel was glad, rather than regretful at this termination to his adventure. He was once more provided with something to do. The re-interment of such bones as this had been his constant care, and he decided at once to restore the bone to consecrated earth. The time seemed opportune. The eyes of the curious were closed in sleep, he himself was still alert and wakeful. The spade remained by his side and the bone in his hand. So he betook himself, there and then, to the churchyard. By the still generous light of the moon, he found a place where the earth yielded to his spade, and within a few minutes the bone was laid decently to earth, some 18 inches deep.

The city clocks struck one as he finished. The whole world seemed asleep, and Mr. Batchel slowly returned to the garden with his spade. As he hung it in its accustomed place he felt stealing over him the welcome desire to sleep. He walked quietly on to the house and ascended to his room. It was now dark: the moon had passed on and left the room in shadow. He lit a candle, and before undressing passed into the library. He had an irresistible curiosity to see the passages in John Evelyn's book which had so strangely adapted themselves to the events of the past hour.

In the library a last surprise awaited him. The desk upon which the book had lain was empty. *The Compleat Gard'ner* stood in its place on the shelf. And then Mr. Batchel knew that he had handled a bone of William Whitehead, and that in response to his own entreaty.

THE WHISPERERS (1912)

Algernon Blackwood (1869–1951)

Algernon Henry Blackwood established a new kind of weird fiction, describing supernatural encounters in which the natural world possesses sinister powers. He was born into a wealthy family, the son of a man who had been a playboy known as "Beauty Blackwood" but who had been converted into a deeply conservative and evangelical Christian during the Crimean War. Blackwood rebelled against his upbringing, becoming interested in mysticism and involved in the Hermetic Order of the Golden Dawn, an occult group that also included Bram Stoker, Arthur Machen and Aleister Crowley as members. His most famous story is 'The Willows', in which two men on a canoeing trip up the Danube stop on an island covered with willows. Blackwood sets up a sense of impending doom by making each natural element on the island seem increasingly malevolent, until it seems that a mystical force is actually attacking the friends.

In addition to fiction exploring the darker side of nature, Blackwood was famed for ghost stories, and in fact featured on the BBC's first ever television programme, *Picture Page*, relating a ghost story at the broadcast from Alexandra Palace on 2 November 1936. He later made regular appearances on both television and radio, and became known as "the Ghost Man".

This is one of his less famous stories, which was first published on 23 May 1912 in *The Eye-Witness*, and reprinted in Blackwood's collection *Ten-Minute Stories* (1914). It deserves to be better known.

TO BE TOO IMPRESSIONABLE IS AS MUCH A SOURCE OF WEAK-
ness as to be hyper-sensitive: so many messages come flooding
in upon one another that confusion is the result; the mind chokes,
imagination grows congested.

Jones, as an imaginative writing man, was well aware of this,
yet could not always prevent it; for if he dulled his mind to one
impression, he ran the risk of blunting it to all. To guard his main
idea, and picket its safe conduct through the seethe of additions that
instantly flocked to join it, was a psychological puzzle that sometimes overtaxed his powers of critical selection. He prepared for it,
however. An editor would ask him for a story—"about five thousand
words, you know"; and Jones would answer, "I'll send it you with
pleasure—when it comes." He knew his difficulty too well to promise more. Ideas were never lacking, but their length of treatment
belonged to machinery he could not coerce. They were alive; they
refused to come to heel to suit mere editors. Midway in a tale that
started crystal clear and definite in its original germ, would pour a
flood of new impressions that either smothered the first conception,
or developed it beyond recognition. Often a short story exfoliated in
this bursting way beyond his power to stop it. He began one, never
knowing where it would lead him. It was ever an adventure. Like
Jack the Giant Killer's beanstalk it grew secretly in the night, fed by
everything he read, saw, felt, or heard. Jones was too impressionable;
he received too many impressions, and too easily.

For this reason, when working at a definite, short idea, he
preferred an empty room, without pictures, furniture, books, or

anything suggestive, and with a skylight that shut out scenery—just ink, blank paper, and the clear picture in his mind. His own interior, unstimulated by the geysers of external life, he made some pretence of regulating; though even under these favourable conditions the matter was not too easy, so prolifically does a sensitive mind engender.

His experience in the empty room of the carpenter's house was a curious case in point—in the little Jura village where his cousin lived to educate his children. "We're all in a pension above the Post Office here," the cousin wrote, "but just now the house is full, and besides is rather noisy. I've taken an attic room for you at the carpenter's near the forest. Some things of mine have been stored there all the winter, but I moved the cases out this morning. There's a bed, writing-table, wash-handstand, sofa, and a skylight window—otherwise empty, as I know you prefer it. You can have your meals with us," etc. And this just suited Jones, who had six weeks' work on hand for which he needed empty solitude. His "idea" was slight and very tender; accretions would easily smother clear presentment; its treatment must be delicate, simple, unconfused.

The room really was an attic, but large, wide, high. He heard the wind rush past the skylight when he went to bed. When the cupboard was open he heard the wind there too, washing the outer walls and tiles. From his pillow he saw a patch of stars peep down upon him. Jones knew the mountains and the woods were close, but he could not see them. Better still, he could not smell them. And he went to bed dead tired, full of his theme for work next morning. He saw it to the end. He could almost have promised five thousand words. With the dawn he would be up and "at it," for he usually woke very early, his mind surcharged, as though subconsciousness had matured the material in sleep. Cold bath, a cup of tea, and then—his writing-table; and the quicker he could reach the writing-table the richer was the content of imaginative thought. What had puzzled him the night before was invariably cleared up in the morning. Only illness could interfere with the process and routine of it.

But this time it was otherwise. He woke, and instantly realised, with a shock of surprise and disappointment, that his mind was— groping. It was groping for his little lost idea. There was nothing physically wrong with him; he felt rested, fresh, clear-headed; but his brain was searching, searching, moreover, in a crowd. Trying to seize hold of the train it had relinquished several hours ago, it caught at an evasive, empty shell. The idea had utterly changed; or rather it seemed smothered by a host of new impressions that came pouring in upon it—new modes of treatment, points of view, in fact development. In the light of these extensions and novel aspects, his original idea had altered beyond recognition. The germ had marvellously exfoliated, so that a whole volume could alone express it. An army of fresh suggestions clamoured for expression. His subconsciousness had grown thick with life; it surged—active, crowded, tumultuous.

And the darkness puzzled him. He remembered the absence of accustomed windows, but it was only when the candle-light brought close the face of his watch, with two o'clock upon it, that he heard the sound of confused whispering in the corners of the room, and realised with a little twinge of fear that those who whispered had just been standing beside his very bed. The room was full.

Though the candle-light proclaimed it empty—bare walls, bare floor, five pieces of unimaginative furniture, and fifty stars peeping through the skylight—it was undeniably thronged with living people whose minds had called him out of heavy sleep. The whispers, of course, died off into the wind that swept the roof and skylight; but the Whisperers remained. They had been trying to get at him; waking suddenly, he had caught them in the very act… And all had brought new interpretations with them; his thought had fundamentally altered; the original idea was snowed under; new images brimmed his mind, and his brain was working as it worked under the high pressure of creative moments.

Jones sat up, trembling a little, and stared about him into the empty room that yet was densely packed with these invisible Whisperers. And he realised this astonishing thing—that he was the object of their deliberate assault, and that scores of other minds, deep, powerful, very active minds, were thundering and beating upon the doors of his imagination. The onset of them was terrific and bewildering, the attack of aggressive ideas obliterating his original story beneath a flood of new suggestions. Inspiration had become suddenly torrential, yet so vast as to be unwieldy, incoherent, useless. It was like the tempest of images that fever brings. His first conception seemed no longer "delicate", but petty. It had turned unreal and tiny, compared with this enormous choice of treatment, extension, development, that now overwhelmed his throbbing brain.

Fear caught vividly at him, as he searched the empty attic-room in vain for explanation. There was absolutely nothing to produce this tempest of new impressions. People seemed talking to him all together, jumbled somewhat, but insistently. It was obsession, rather than inspiration; and so bitingly, dreadfully real.

"Who are you all?" his mind whispered to blank walls and vacant corners.

Back from the shouting floor and ceiling came the chorus of images that stormed and clamoured for expression. Jones lay still and listened; he let them come. There was nothing else to do. He lay fearful, negative, receptive. It was all too big for him to manage, set to some scale of high achievement that submerged his own small powers. It came, too, in a series of impressions, all separate, yet all somehow interwoven.

In vain he tried to sort them out and sift them. As well sort out waves upon an agitated sea. They were too self-assertive for direction or control. Like wild animals, hungry, thirsty, ravening, they rushed from every side and fastened on his mind.

Yet he perceived them in a certain sequence.

For, first, the unfurnished attic-chamber was full of human passion, of love and hate, revenge and wicked cunning, of jealousy, courage, cowardice, of every vital human emotion ever longed for, enjoyed, or frustrated, all clamouring for—expression.

Flaming across and through these, incongruously threaded in and out, ran next a yearning softness of incredible beauty that sighed in the empty spaces of his heart, pleading for impossible fulfilment...

And, after these, carrying both one and other upon their surface, huge questions flashed and dived and thundered in a patterned, wild entanglement, calling to be unravelled and made straight. Moreover, with every set came a new suggested treatment of the little clear idea he had taken to bed with him five hours before.

Jones adopted each in turn. Imagination writhed and twisted beneath the stress of all these potential modes of expression he must choose between. His small idea exfoliated into many volumes, work enough to fill a dozen lives. It was most gorgeously exhilarating, though so hopelessly unmanageable. He felt like many minds in one...

Then came another chain of impressions, violent, yet steady owing to their depth; the voices, questions, pleadings turned to pictures; and he saw, struggling through the deeps of him, enormous quantities of people, passing along like rivers, massed, herded, swayed here and there by some outstanding figure of command who directed them like flowing water. They shrieked, and fought, and battled, then sank out of sight, huddled and destroyed in—blood…

And their places were taken instantly by white crowds with shining eyes, and yearning in their faces, who climbed precipitous heights towards some Radiance that kept ever out of sight, like sunrise behind mountains that clouds then swallow… The pelt and thunder of images was destructive in its torrent; his little, first idea was drowned and wrecked… Jones sank back exhausted, utterly dismayed. He gave up all attempt to make selection.

The driving storm swept through him, on and on, now waxing, now waning, but never growing less, and apparently endless as the sky. It rushed in circles, like the turning of a giant wheel. All the activities that human minds have ever battled with since thought began came booming, crashing, straining for expression against the imaginative stuff whereof his mind was built. The walls began to yield and settle. It was like the chaos that madness brings. He did not struggle against it; he let it come, lying open and receptive, pliant and plastic to every detail of the vast invasion. And the only time he attempted a complete obedience, reaching out for the pencil and notebook that lay beside his bed, he desisted instantly again, sinking back upon his pillows with a kind of frightened laughter. For the tempest seemed then to knock him down and bruise his very brain. Inextricable confusion caught him. He might as well have tried to make notes of the entire Alexandrian Library in half an hour…

Then, most singular of all, as he felt the sleep of exhaustion fall upon his tired nerves, he heard that deep, prodigious sound. All that had preceded, it gathered marvellously in, mothering it with a sweetness that seemed to his imagination like some harmonious, geometrical skein including all the activities men's minds have ever known. Faintly he realised it only, discerned from infinitely far away. Into the streams of apparent contradiction that warred so strenuously about him, it seemed to bring some hint of unifying, harmonious explanation… And, here and there, as sleep buried him, he imagined that chords lay threaded along strings of cadences, breaking sometimes even into melody—music that rose everywhere from life and wove Thought into a homogeneous Whole…

"Sleep well?" his cousin inquired, when he appeared very late next day for *déjeuner*. "Think you'll be able to work in that room all right?"

"I slept, yes, thanks," said Jones. "No doubt I shall work there right enough—when I'm rested. By the bye," he asked presently, "what has the attic been used for lately? What's been in it, I mean?"

"Books, only books," was the reply. "I've stored my 'library' there for months, without a chance of using it. I move about so much, you see. Five hundred books were taken out just before you came. I often think," he added lightly, "that when books are unopened like that for long, the minds that wrote them must get restless and—"

"What sort of books were they?" Jones interrupted.

"Fiction, poetry, philosophy, history, religion, music. I've got two hundred books on music alone."

FINGERS OF A HAND (1920)

H.D. Everett (1851–1923)

Henrietta Dorothy Everett, who usually wrote under the pen name Theo Douglas, was a hugely popular novelist during her life but has since been almost entirely forgotten. Her identity was revealed in 1910, and this story was published in her ghost story collection *The Death-Mask, and Other Ghosts* (1920), under her own name. M.R. James praised the book in his essay 'Some remarks on Ghost Stories' (1929), describing it as "of a rather quieter tone on the whole, but with some excellently conceived stories".

The epigraph at the start of this story is a quote from the King James Bible, referring to the story of Belshazzar's Feast, where the king receives a warning through mysterious writing that appears on the wall.

"In the same hour came forth
the fingers of a man's hand and wrote...
and the king saw the part of the hand that wrote."

T HE CHILDREN WERE SUPPOSED TO NEED A SEASIDE CHANGE, and I daresay they did, poor wee things, as they had had whooping-cough in the spring, and measles to follow. As you know, we are taking care of them for Bernard, who is in India with his wife, and so we are even more anxious about them than if they were our own. That is one great use of unmarried aunts— to shoulder other people's responsibilities; and I, for one, think the world would be a poorer place if the "million of unwanted women" were, by some convulsion of nature, to be swept away. I only mention the children's measles as the reason why we took those lodgings at Cove at the beginning of July, for, now one has to economise, we should not have gone in for a seaside change as a luxury for ourselves.

The lodgings were clean and fairly comfortable, and we took them for two months certain, letting our own pretty cottage in the Midlands for a similar term. And that was why we had no home of our own to retreat to when—But I am telling my story upside down, as Sara says I always do. You would not be likely to understand, if I did not begin in the right place, with what went before.

The house was Number Seven, Cliff Terrace, a row of detached villas above the road, on the other side of which was the esplanade and the sea. There were no other lodgers, as we took both Mrs. Mills's "sets"; nobody in the house but ourselves and the bairns, and that important person Nurse, except Mrs.

Mills herself, and her daughter who waited on us. So you see there was no one who could have played tricks—But again I am getting on too fast.

We had never been to Cove before, or to St. Eanswyth either, the larger watering-place which lies to the east of Cove; but we thought our choice of place for a summer holiday was amply justified by the pretty inland neighbourhood and the sweet air, and a safe beach close at hand, where the children could be out playing early and late under the guardian wing of Nurse. For the first fortnight we were all satisfied and happy, and, both in metaphor and actually, there was not a cloud in the sky.

Then the rain began, not brief summer showers and sunshine in between, but the worst weather of a wet July—a continuous downpour with hardly ten minutes intermission, and going on for days: such rain as Noah must have witnessed before the beginning of the Flood.

Of course the poor children had to keep to the house, and, though they and Nurse had the dining-room set to themselves, there was but little space for them to play about. Sara and I occupied the drawing-room, and she had been sketching from the window—not that there was much visible to make into a picture: a leaden sea and slanting lines of rain, and boats drawn up on the beach. At last she pushed away colour-box and pencils.

"I can't stand this any longer," she said. "Rain or no rain, I am going out. It will be a good opportunity to test the resisting powers of my new cloak. You must stay in to-day, as I believe you have caught cold."

I did not dispute her fiat. Sara always decides what is, or what is not to be done, and I, who am a biddable person, submit to be ruled. And, to say the truth, I was not particularly anxious to get wet. I went on with my sewing till it was nearly time for Miss Mills to appear with the luncheon-tray, and then I began to clear the table of Sara's scattered possessions.

Some blank sheets of paper were lying about, besides the one pinned to her board with the half-finished sketch; and on one of these I noticed some large scrawled writing. Not Sara's writing, which is particularly small and neat; not the writing of any one I knew. The words were quite legible, but they were very odd. GO—by itself at the top of the sheet; and the same word repeated twice below, followed by GET OUT AT ONCE.

Of course I showed Sara this when she came in to luncheon, and she could not account for it any more than I. The sheets were unmarked when she took them out of her portfolio; of that she seemed to be certain.

"Some one has been playing a trick on us," she said. "If it is Mrs. Mills, it is an odd sort of notice"; and at this very mild witticism both of us laughed.

But the idea of a trick being played was absurd: I had been in the room the whole time, as I said.

"Unless you think I dozed off while you were out, and did it in my sleep!"

Sara laughed again, and began to sort the loose papers back into place.

"Why, here is more of it," she exclaimed; and I saw on the sheet she held out, in the same large scrawl, a repetition of the words—GET OUT—GET OUT AT ONCE.

Now I could have sworn—had swearing been of any use—that I had looked those papers over on both sides after finding the first writing, and with that sole exception they bore no mark whatever. So these last words must have been written after my discovery and before Sara's return, and while I was beside them in the room. Surely they had been traced by no mortal hand!

You will not wonder that such a curious happening was the subject of discussion between us during the rest of that wet day. "I'd give anything to know who did it," Sara was saying, while I added: "I should like better still to know what it means." I am more credulous than Sara, and it seemed to me there must be some meaning in anything so unaccountable. I had this feeling from the very first, and, as you will see, both the conviction and the reason for it grew.

I pass on to the following Sunday. The weather was still wet, and the children were kept mainly to the house. For the sake of variety for them, Sara had little Dick and Nancy upstairs in our sitting-room for their Sunday lessons, which as a rule devolve on her to give, as she is a cleverer teacher than I. Lessons of the simplest, as they generally consist of showing pictures and giving explanations; and to be allowed to look at Sara's illustrated Bible is a frequent Sabbath treat. The children had gone down again to Nurse, and Sara was about to tidy the book away, when she gave a sharp exclamation.

"Grace, look here. Who can have done this?"

The volume was lying open at the nineteenth chapter of Genesis, and these words in the twenty-second verse were scored under blackly in pencil—*Haste thee: escape.*

Now Sara, who is particular in everything, is especially so about her books. She hates any soil or mark upon them, and nothing irritates her more than to have a lent volume returned with "purple passages" scored beside in the margin, whether in approval or otherwise. "Tut-tut," she was saying, at the usual pitch of exasperation. "It is really unpardonable. *Where* is my india-rubber? I must see if I can take it out. It could not have been the children. And the Millses would never—! But there is nobody else."

"You would have seen, had it been the children. They are good little things, and would not: besides, they had not a pencil"—(thus I weakened an argument based on their righteousness). "And what odd words to have chosen to mark, when you think of the other scrawls. I wonder if this is all. It is possible there may be more."

"I shall look the book right through and see, and then I shall lock it in my box."

Sara sat down to her task armed with the piece of rubber, and by no means in a Sabbath spirit of peace and good-will. She did find two other texts scored under, and these were the marked words:

2 Kings, ninth chapter and third verse. *Open the door and flee and tarry not.*

St. Matthew, seventh chapter and twenty-seventh verse. *The... house... fell, and great was the fall thereof.*

I was superstitious, because disturbed by these happenings. So I was told, yet who would not have been affected in my place? I believe Sara too was disquieted in her secret mind, though she would not allow it. But then she was used to pride herself on being an *esprit fort*.

I kept saying to myself, What next?—and the next came quickly. I did not tell Sara what I purposed doing, but I left a couple of sheets of paper and a freshly cut pencil displayed on the table when we were going out. More writing might be done with the opportunity given, and "it" might vouchsafe to make clear "its" meaning. I could not then have analysed what I meant by the convenient impersonal pronoun, nor am I clear of the exact meaning now.

We were about to do some shopping in the town, and I had stupidly left my purse on the mantel-shelf in the sitting-room, so I was obliged to turn back to get it. As I opened the door, my eyes fell at once upon the papers, and I saw some dark object moving across the white surface, and then quickly disappearing over the table edge. It was too big for a mouse; could it have been a rat? The thought of a rat gave me a nervous shiver; I think I would have a greater terror of rats than of ghosts. I looked at the papers though I did not touch them; yes, a vague scrawl was begun upon the upper one, not developed into legible words. I had disturbed the writer too soon. But what could the writer be, coming in the form of a rat, or the shadow of a rat, and yet able to write words which appeared to convey a message? I left the papers as they were, but the scrawl was not continued; no doubt that unexpected first return had scared away the writer.

I said nothing to Sara of my failed experiment; but next day about the same time I laid my trap again, this time staying in the room, but retired into a distant corner, where I set myself to watch.

For a long while there was nothing. Then an object ill-defined and shadowy crept across the paper, stealing towards the pencil as it lay. I hardly dared breathe, the excitement was so tense. Over the pencil this shadow paused, and now became denser, taking solid form. It was not the whole of a hand, but a thumb and two fingers, forming something like a claw. But, if you consider, a thumb and two fingers are all a hand needs to manipulate a pencil, and "it" may not have cared to materialise anything superfluous. The pencil now slanted upwards between these fingers and the thumb, and—yes, no doubt remained—the claw was writing. Now we would know all, such was my sanguine thought, not forecasting how deep the mystery would remain.

It was Sara this time who interrupted, coming in. The pencil dropped, the claw from a solid form became a shadow, and slipped away over the edge of the table, as I had seen it vanish before. Sara noticed nothing; she was too full of her news, and of the letter open in her hand.

"Look at this. We ought to have had it two days ago, but there was a mistake in the address. It is from Mrs. Bernard's mother" (Mrs. Bernard is our brother's wife). "She is at Diplake for ten days before they go to Scotland, and she wants one of us to bring the children there just for the time they stay. She says she is sorry she cannot have us both, but it is a case of a single room, as the house is full. She is expecting us to-morrow, so I shall have to wire, and tell Nurse to get ready. Will you go, Grace, or shall I?"

"Of course you must be the one. I should never get on at Diplake, and with a large, gay party. You must go, Sara, and put your best foot foremost, for Bernard's sake. And—I'm glad you have to take the children. For look what is written here!"

I showed her the paper on which the claw had scrawled. Over and over again the word DANGER, as if it could not be too often insisted on. Then, also repeated: GO. GET OUT. Then an attempt at *children*, afterwards clearly written: DANGER. CHILDREN MUST GO.

I think Sara was impressed at last, though she hardly believed in the claw I had seen writing. As to that, I must—she said—have been hallucinated, or else slept and dreamed. But little time remained for argument, as all was in a hurry of preparation—boxes to be packed, and the children to be consoled, for their enjoyment of the seaside pleasures was very keen, and the attraction small of going to stay with an almost unknown grandmother. "But we are coming back?" said little Nancy. "We are coming back again here?" I believe I told her yes, but as to what will happen in the future, who can say?

They set out early next morning, Sara and the three children and Nurse, and I saw them off at the station. Sara said almost at the last:

"I don't half like leaving you alone here, Grace. If you find the lodgings too solitary, why not take a room at the hotel for the days I am away?"

I said I would think of it, but in truth I felt no special nervousness or concern, only an intense curiosity to see what would happen now we had (by pure accident) obeyed the dictation of the writing, and sent the children away.

The lonely evening passed for me without disturbance; Miss Mills came at the usual time to carry down my supper tray, and wished me good-night, and shortly after this I went to bed.

I slept, and do not remember any warning dreams. But in the very early daylight I was suddenly startled broad awake—not I think by any noise, but by an alteration in the level of my bed. My head was low, almost on the floor, and my feet were high in air. Everything in the room was sliding and altering; basin and ewer slipped from the washstand, crashed and broke, and pictures flapped from the wall. Then came a greater crash like the jolting of a thunder-clap, and it was close at hand; chimney-pots falling, walls and roofs collapsing: was it an earthquake that had happened? I heard screams and shouts, but the sliding movement had stopped.

I struggled up and to my feet, for I had been half buried by the bedclothes falling back upon me; and there opposite was a great crack or rent in the outer wall, wide enough to admit my arm, with the new morning looking through, and a waft of air blowing in keenly from the sea. It was as if the house had broken in two. What but an earthquake could have caused such a disaster?—and again I heard people screaming. The often repeated warning, the scored words in the Bible ran in my head. I could be thankful indeed that Sara and the children were safe at Diplake out of the way: what an agony had they been still here, and those screams possibly theirs!

I do not know how long it took me to scramble up the slanting floor, to find my clothes, my shoes, where all was confusion, so that if it were possible to get out of the house I might go forth clad. Then I tried the door.

It was in some way jammed, and it seemed as if ages passed before I could wrench it open. When at last it gave way, the wreck revealed without was worse than the wreck within. The staircase was a heap of broken wood, and the back wall had fallen inwards; there was no getting down that way. What had become, I wondered, of Mrs. Mills and her daughter, and was it their screams that I heard? I called to them by name, but there was no answer.

Baffled so, I looked from the window, which had hardly a whole pane left. It was as if the terrace had disappeared: the road was broken up, and the house had been carried down with the sliding earth, many yards nearer the sea. A crowd had assembled, staring at this phenomenon, but at a safe distance. I shouted to them, and a man called up to me instructions to stay where I was, as a ladder would presently be brought.

I knew later that they feared at first to touch the house, lest it should collapse in total ruin like the one next on the terrace, where, alas! two people had been killed, overwhelmed and buried in their sleep.

This was a danger indeed, about which that warning came. The part of our house which fell, was where the children would have been sleeping. I was told that tons and tons of masonry had crushed in their little beds; even now it makes me sick to think of what we so narrowly escaped. The Millses, mother and daughter, were dug out of the basement quite unharmed, but I am afraid, poor people, they are heavy losers. I myself had not a scratch.

The great landslip at Cove, with all its damage and disaster, will surely pass into history: the slide of the undercliff down into the sea, the gaping fissure torn above, hundreds of feet in length—the alteration of the ground below, heaped into mounds and billows like the waves of the sea, while the buildings in the course of the slide are broken up and displaced like a set of children's toys, playthings in the hands of a giant. People who are wise about the geological formation, talk of a bed of slippery clay underlying the upper strata, and say water had percolated down to it owing to the wet spring, and, following upon that, the heavy rains of that dismal week in July. But they are wise after the event and did not forecast it: indeed it was anticipated by no one other than the writer of those mysterious words.

THE NATURE OF THE EVIDENCE (1923)

May Sinclair (1863–1946)

A modernist writer, Mary Amelia St. Clair (May Sinclair) was inspired by the works of Sigmund Freud and incorporated psychoanalytical theory into both her ghost stories and her more mainstream novels and stories. She had a tragic early life—her alcoholic father died when she was in her teens, and all her five brothers died young, four of them from heart failure. She never married but took on responsibility for the children of two of her dead brothers. In addition to her long interest in psychology, and her involvement in the fight for women's rights and suffrage, Sinclair was also a member of the Society of Psychical Research, which conducted scientific studies into paranormal activities. All these interests are brought together in her two collections of ghostly fiction, *Uncanny Stories* (1923), in which 'The Nature of the Evidence' appeared, and *The Intercessor, and Other Stories* (1931).

Uncanny Stories deals with the broad theme of the suitability of love. 'The Nature of the Evidence', in which a man's unsuitable second marriage to the lascivious Pauline is doomed by the ghostly presence of his first wife, is a sort of inverted precursor to Daphne du Maurier's classic novel *Rebecca* (1938). In the story, Pauline hates the house's library, not realising that it is haunted by the memory—and perhaps more than the memory—of her predecessor.

T HIS IS THE STORY MARSTON TOLD ME. HE DIDN'T WANT TO
tell it. I had to tear it from him bit by bit. I've pieced the bits
together in their time order, and explained things here and there,
but the facts are the facts he gave me. There's nothing that I didn't
get out of him somehow.

Out of *him*—you'll admit my source is unimpeachable. Edward
Marston, the great K.C., and the author of an admirable work on
The Logic of Evidence. You should have read the chapters on "What
Evidence Is and What It Is Not". You may say he lied; but if you
knew Marston you'd know he wouldn't lie, for the simple reason
that he's incapable of inventing anything. So that, if you ask me
whether I believe this tale, all I can say is, I believe the things happened, because he said they happened and because they happened
to him. As for what they *were*—well, I don't pretend to explain it,
neither would he.

You know he was married twice. He adored his first wife,
Rosamund, and Rosamund adored him. I suppose they were completely happy. She was fifteen years younger than he, and beautiful.
I wish I could make you see how beautiful. Her eyes and mouth
had the same sort of bow, full and wide-sweeping, and they stared
out of her face with the same grave, contemplative innocence.
Her mouth was finished off at each corner with the loveliest little
moulding, rounded like the pistil of a flower. She wore her hair in
a solid gold fringe over her forehead, like a child's, and a big coil
at the back. When it was let down it hung in a heavy cable to her
waist. Marston used to tease her about it. She had a trick of tossing

back the rope in the night when it was hot under her, and it would fall smack across his face and hurt him.

There was a pathos about her that I can't describe—a curious, pure, sweet beauty, like a child's; perfect, and perfectly immature; so immature that you couldn't conceive its lasting—like that—any more than childhood lasts. Marston used to say it made him nervous. He was afraid of waking up in the morning and finding that it had changed in the night And her beauty was so much a part of herself that you couldn't think of her without it. Somehow you felt that if it went she must go too.

Well, she went first.

For a year afterwards Marston existed dangerously, always on the edge of a break-down. If he didn't go over altogether it was because his work saved him. He had no consoling theories. He was one of those bigoted materialists of the nineteenth-century type who believe that consciousness is a purely physiological function, and that when your body's dead, *you're* dead. He saw no reason to suppose the contrary. "When you consider," he used to say, "the nature of the evidence!"

It's as well to bear this in mind, so as to realise that he hadn't any bias or anticipation. Rosamund survived for him only in his memory. And in his memory he was still in love with her. At the same time he used to discuss quite cynically the chances of his marrying again.

It seems that in their honeymoon they had gone into that. Rosamund said she hated to think of his being lonely and miserable, supposing she died before he did. She would like him to marry again. If, she stipulated, he married the right woman.

He had put it to her: "And if I marry the wrong one?"

And she had said, That would be different. She couldn't bear that.

He remembered all this afterwards; but there was nothing in it to make him suppose, at the time, that she would take action.

We talked it over, he and I, one night.

"I suppose," he said, "I shall have to marry again. It's a physical necessity. But it won't be anything more. I shan't marry the sort of woman who'll expect anything more. I won't put another woman in Rosamund's place. There'll be no unfaithfulness about it."

And there wasn't. Soon after that first year he married Pauline Silver.

She was a daughter of old Justice Parker, who was a friend of Marston's people. He hadn't seen the girl till she came home from India after her divorce.

Yes, there'd been a divorce. Silver had behaved very decently. He'd let her bring it against *him,* to save her. But there were some queer stories going about. They didn't get round to Marston, because he was so mixed up with her people; and if they had he wouldn't have believed them. He'd made up his mind he'd marry Pauline the first minute he'd seen her. She was handsome; the hard, black, white and vermilion kind, with a little aristocratic nose and a lascivious mouth.

It was, as he had meant it to be, nothing but physical infatuation on both sides. No question of Pauline's taking Rosamund's place.

Marston had a big case on at the time.

They were in such a hurry that they couldn't wait till it was over; and as it kept him in London they agreed to put off their honeymoon till the autumn, and he took her straight to his own house in Curzon Street.

This, he admitted afterwards, was the part he hated. The Curzon Street house was associated with Rosamund; especially their bed-room—Rosamund's bedroom—and his library. The library was the room Rosamund liked best, because it was his room. She had her place in the corner by the hearth, and they were always alone there together in the evenings when his work was done, and when it wasn't done she would still sit with him, keeping quiet in her corner with a book.

Luckily for Marston, at the first sight of the library Pauline took a dislike to it.

I can hear her. "Br-rr-rh! There's something beastly about this room, Edward. I can't think how you can sit in it."

And Edward, a little caustic:

"*You* needn't, if you don't like it."

"I certainly shan't."

She stood there—I can see her—on the hearthrug by Rosamund's chair, looking uncommonly handsome and lascivious. He was going to take her in his arms and kiss her vermilion mouth, when, he said, something stopped him. Stopped him clean, as if it had risen up and stepped between them. He supposed it was the memory of Rosamund, vivid in the place that had been hers.

You see it was just that place, of silent, intimate communion, that Pauline would never take. And the rich, coarse, contented creature didn't even want to take it. He saw that he would be left alone there, all right, with his memory.

But the bedroom was another matter. That, Pauline had made it understood from the beginning, she would have to have. Indeed, there was no other he could well have offered her. The drawing-room covered the whole of the first floor. The bedrooms above were cramped, and this one had been formed by throwing the two front rooms into one. It looked south, and the bathroom opened out of it at the back. Marston's small northern room had a door on the narrow landing at right angles to his wife's door. He could hardly expect her to sleep there, still less in any of the tight boxes on the top floor. He said he wished he had sold the Curzon Street house.

But Pauline was enchanted with the wide, three-windowed piece that was to be hers. It had been exquisitely furnished for poor little Rosamund; all seventeenth-century walnut wood, Bokhara rugs, thick silk curtains, deep blue with purple linings, and a big, rich bed covered with a purple counterpane embroidered in blue.

One thing Marston insisted on: that *he* should sleep on Rosamund's side of the bed, and Pauline in his own old place. He didn't want to see Pauline's body where Rosamund's had been. Of course he had to lie about it and pretend he had always slept on the side next the window.

I can see Pauline going about in that room, looking at everything; looking at herself, her black, white and vermilion, in the glass that had held Rosamund's pure rose and gold; opening the wardrobe where Rosamund's dresses used to hang, sniffing up the delicate, flower scent of Rosamund, not caring, covering it with her own thick trail.

And Marston (who cared abominably)—I can see him getting more miserable and at the same time more excited as the wedding evening went on. He took her to the play to fill up the time, or perhaps to get her out of Rosamund's rooms; God knows. I can see them sitting in the stalls, bored and restless, starting up and going out before the thing was half over, and coming back to that house in Curzon Street before eleven o'clock.

It wasn't much past eleven when he went to her room.

I told you her door was at right angles to his, and the landing was narrow, so that anybody standing by Pauline's door must have been seen the minute he opened his. He hadn't even to cross the landing to get to her.

Well, Marston swears that there was nothing there when he opened his own door; but when he came to Pauline's he saw Rosamund standing up before it; and, he said, *"She wouldn't let me in."*

Her arms were stretched out, barring the passage. Oh yes, he saw her face, Rosamund's face; I gathered that it was utterly sweet, and utterly inexorable. He couldn't pass her.

So he turned into his own room, backing, he says, so that he could keep looking at her. And when he stood on the threshold of his own door she wasn't there.

No, he wasn't frightened. He couldn't tell me what he felt; but he left his door open all night because he couldn't bear to shut it on her. And he made no other attempt to go in to Pauline; he was so convinced that the phantasm of Rosamund would come again and stop him.

I don't know what sort of excuse he made to Pauline the next morning. He said she was very stiff and sulky all day; and no wonder. He was still infatuated with her, and I don't think that the phantasm of Rosamund had put him off Pauline in the least. In fact, he persuaded himself that the thing was nothing but a hallucination, due, no doubt, to his excitement.

Anyhow, he didn't expect to see it at the door again the next night.

Yes. It was there. Only, this time, he said, it drew aside to let him pass. It smiled at him, as if it were saying, "Go in, if you must; you'll see what'll happen."

He had no sense that it had followed him into the room; he felt certain that, this time, it would let him be.

It was when he approached Pauline's bed, which had been Rosamund's bed, that she appeared again, standing between it and him, and stretching out her arms to keep him back.

All that Pauline could see was her bridegroom backing and backing, then standing there, fixed, and the look on his face. That in itself was enough to frighten her.

She said, "What's the matter with you, Edward?"

He didn't move.

"What are you standing there for? Why don't you come to bed?"

Then Marston seems to have lost his head and blurted it out: "I can't. I can't."

"Can't what?" said Pauline from the bed.

"Can't sleep with you. She won't let me."

"She?"

"Rosamund. My wife. She's there."

"What on earth are you talking about?"

"She's there, I tell you. She won't let me. She's pushing me back."

He says Pauline must have thought he was drunk or something. Remember, she *saw* nothing but Edward, his face, and his mysterious attitude. He must have looked very drunk.

She sat up in bed, with her hard, black eyes blazing away at him, and told him to leave the room that minute. Which he did.

The next day she had it out with him. I gathered that she kept on talking about the "state" he was in.

"You came to my room, Edward, in a *disgraceful* state."

I suppose Marston said he was sorry; but he couldn't help it; he wasn't drunk. He stuck to it that Rosamund was there. He had seen her. And Pauline said, if he wasn't drunk then he must be mad, and he said meekly, "Perhaps I *am* mad."

That set her off, and she broke out in a fury. He was no more mad than she was; but he didn't care for her; he was making ridiculous excuses; shamming, to put her off. There was some other woman.

Marston asked her what on earth she supposed he'd married her for. Then she burst out crying and said she didn't know.

Then he seems to have made it up with Pauline. He managed to make her believe he wasn't lying, that he really had seen something, and between them they arrived at a rational explanation of the appearance. He had been overworking. Rosamund's phantasm was nothing but a hallucination of his exhausted brain.

This theory carried him on till bed-time. Then, he says, he began to wonder what would happen, what Rosamund's phantasm would do next. Each morning his passion for Pauline had come back again, increased by frustration, and it worked itself up crescendo, towards night. Supposing he *had* seen Rosamund. He might see her again. He had become suddenly subject to hallucinations. But as long as you *knew* you were hallucinated you were all right.

So what they agreed to do that night was by way of precaution, in case the thing came again. It might even be sufficient in itself to prevent his seeing anything.

Instead of going in to Pauline he was to get into the room before she did, and she was to come to him there. That, they said, would break the spell. To make him feel even safer he meant to be in bed before Pauline came.

Well, he got into the room all right.

It was when he tried to get into bed that—he saw her (I mean Rosamund).

She was lying there, in his place next the window, her own place, lying in her immature child-like beauty and sleeping, the firm full bow of her mouth softened by sleep. She was perfect in every detail, the lashes of her shut eyelids golden on her white cheeks, the solid gold of her square fringe shining, and the great braided golden rope of her hair flung back on the pillow.

He knelt down by the bed and pressed his forehead into the bedclothes, close to her side. He declared he could feel her breathe.

He stayed there for the twenty minutes Pauline took to undress and come to him. He says the minutes stretched out like hours. Pauline found him still kneeling with his face pressed into the bedclothes. When he got up he staggered.

She asked him what he was doing and why he wasn't in bed. And he said. "It's no use. I can't. I can't."

But somehow he couldn't tell her that Rosamund was there. Rosamund was too sacred; he couldn't talk about her. He only said:

"You'd better sleep in my room to-night."

He was staring down at the place in the bed where he still saw Rosamund. Pauline couldn't have seen anything but the bedclothes, the sheet smoothed above an invisible breast, and the hollow in the pillow. She said she'd do nothing of the sort. She wasn't going to be frightened out of her own room. He could do as he liked.

He couldn't leave them there; he couldn't leave Pauline with Rosamund, and he couldn't leave Rosamund with Pauline. So he sat up in a chair with his back turned to the bed. No. He didn't make any attempt to go back. He says he knew she was still lying there, guarding his place, which was her place. The odd thing is that he wasn't in the least disturbed or frightened or surprised. He took the whole thing as a matter of course. And presently he dozed off into a sleep.

A scream woke him and the sound of a violent body leaping out of the bed and thudding on to its feet. He switched on the light and saw the bedclothes flung back and Pauline standing on the floor with her mouth open.

He went to her and held her. She was cold to the touch and shaking with terror, and her jaws dropped as if she was palsied.

She said, "Edward, there's something in the bed."

He glanced again at the bed. It was empty.

"There isn't," he said. "Look."

He stripped the bed to the foot-rail, so that she could see.

"There *was* something."

"Do you see it."

"No. I felt it."

She told him. First something had come swinging, smack across her face. A thick, heavy rope of woman's hair. It had waked her. Then she had put out her hands and felt the body. A woman's body, soft and horrible; her fingers had sunk in the shallow breasts. Then she had screamed and jumped.

And she couldn't stay in the room. The room, she said, was "beastly".

She slept in Marston's room, in his small single bed, and he sat up with her all night, on a chair.

She believed now that he had really seen something, and she remembered that the library was beastly, too. Haunted by something. She supposed that was what she had felt. Very well. Two rooms in the house were haunted; their bedroom and the library. They would just have to avoid those two rooms. She had made up her mind, you see, that it was nothing but a case of an ordinary haunted house; the sort of thing you're always hearing about and never believe in till it happens to yourself. Marston didn't like to point out to her that the house hadn't been haunted till she came into it.

The following night, the fourth night, she was to sleep in the spare room on the top floor, next to the servants, and Marston in his own room.

But Marston didn't sleep. He kept on wondering whether he would or would not go up to Pauline's room. That made him horribly restless, and instead of undressing and going to bed, he sat up on a chair with a book. He wasn't nervous; but he had a queer feeling that something was going to happen, and that he must be ready for it, and that he'd better be dressed.

It must have been soon after midnight when he heard the door knob turning very slowly and softly.

The door opened behind him and Pauline came in, moving without a sound, and stood before him. It gave him a shock; for he had been thinking of Rosamund, and when he heard the door knob turn it was the phantasm of Rosamund that he expected to see coming in. He says, for the first minute, it was this appearance of Pauline that struck him as the uncanny and unnatural thing.

She had nothing, absolutely nothing on but a transparent white chiffony sort of dressing-gown. She was trying to undo it. He could see her hands shaking as her fingers fumbled with the fastenings.

He got up suddenly, and they just stood there before each other, saying nothing, staring at each other. He was fascinated by her, by the sheer glamour of her body, gleaming white through the thin stuff, and by the movement of her fingers. I think I've said she was a beautiful woman, and her beauty at that moment was overpowering.

And still he stared at her without saying anything. It sounds as if their silence lasted quite a long time, but in reality it couldn't have been more than some fraction of a second.

Then she began. "Oh, Edward, for God's sake *say* something. Oughtn't I to have come?"

And she went on without waiting for an answer. "Are you thinking of *her*? Because, if—if you are, I'm not going to let her drive you away from me... I'm not going to... She'll keep on coming as long as we don't—Can't you see that this is the way to stop it...? When you take me in your arms."

She slipped off the loose sleeves of the chiffon thing and it fell to her feet. Marston says he heard a queer sound, something between a groan and a grunt, and was amazed to find that it came from himself.

He hadn't touched her yet—mind you, it went quicker than it takes to tell, it was still an affair of the fraction of a second—they were holding out their arms to each other, when the door opened again without a sound, and, without visible passage, the phantasm was there. It came incredibly fast, and thin at first, like a shaft of light sliding between them. It didn't do anything; there was no beating of hands, only, as it took on its full form, its perfect likeness of flesh and blood, it made its presence felt like a push, a force, driving them asunder.

Pauline hadn't seen it yet. She thought it was Marston who was beating her back. She cried out: "Oh, don't, don't push me away!" She stooped below the phantasm's guard and clung to his knees, writhing and crying. For a moment it was a struggle between her moving flesh and that still, supernatural being.

And in that moment Marston realised that he hated Pauline. She was fighting Rosamund with her gross flesh and blood, taking a mean advantage of her embodied state to beat down the heavenly, discarnate thing.

He called to her to let go.

"It's not I," he shouted. "Can't you *see* her?"

Then, suddenly, she saw, and let go, and dropped, crouching on the floor and trying to cover herself. This time she had given no cry.

The phantasm gave way; it moved slowly towards the door, and as it went it looked back over its shoulder at Marston, it trailed a hand, signalling to him to come.

He went out after it, hardly aware of Pauline's naked body that still writhed there, clutching at his feet as they passed, and drew itself after him, like a worm, like a beast, along the floor.

She must have got up at once and followed them out on to the landing; for, as he went down the stairs behind the phantasm, he could see Pauline's face, distorted with lust and terror, peering at them above the stairhead. She saw them descend the last flight, and cross the hall at the bottom and go into the library. The door shut behind them.

Something happened in there. Marston never told me precisely what it was, and I didn't ask him. Anyhow, that finished it.

The next day Pauline ran away to her own people. She couldn't stay in Marston's house because it was haunted by Rosamund, and he wouldn't leave it for the same reason.

And she never came back; for she was not only afraid of Rosamund, she was afraid of Marston. And if she *had* come it wouldn't have been any good. Marston was convinced that, as often as he attempted to get to Pauline, something would stop him. Pauline certainly felt that, if Rosamund were pushed to it, she might show herself in some still more sinister and terrifying form. She knew when she was beaten.

And there was more in it than that. I believe he tried to explain it to her; said he had married her on the assumption that Rosamund was dead, but that now he knew she was alive; she was, as he put it, "there". He tried to make her see that if he had Rosamund he couldn't have *her*. Rosamund's presence in the world annulled the contract.

You see I'm convinced that something *did* happen that night in the library. I say, he never told me precisely what it was, but he once let something out. We were discussing one of Pauline's love-affairs (after the separation she gave him endless grounds for divorce).

"Poor Pauline," he said, "she thinks she's so passionate."

"Well," I said, "wasn't she?"

Then he burst out. "No. She doesn't know what passion is. None of you know. You haven't the faintest conception. You'd have to get rid of your bodies first. I didn't know until—"

He stopped himself. I think he was going to say, "until Rosamund came back and showed me". For he leaned forward and whispered: "It isn't a localised affair at all... If you only knew—"

So I don't think it was just faithfulness to a revived memory. I take it there had been, behind that shut door, some experience, some terrible and exquisite contact. More penetrating than sight or touch. More—more extensive: passion at all points of being.

Perhaps the supreme moment of it, the ecstasy, only came when her phantasm had disappeared.

He couldn't go back to Pauline after *that*.

MR. TALLENT'S GHOST (1926)

Mary Webb (1881–1927)

Mary Webb is best known today for her novels of the Shropshire countryside, such as *Gone to Earth* (1917) and *Precious Bane* (1924). She spent most of her life as an invalid suffering from Graves' disease, and felt keenly the pain of others too. As well as tremendous generosity towards the poor (even when semi-impoverished herself), she vehemently opposed blood sports and was a vegetarian. Her novels are passionate and tragic, and although she never achieved real fame in her lifetime, a year after her premature death the prime minister Stanley Baldwin gave a speech in her praise at the Royal Literary Fund dinner, and her popularity grew.

In total contrast to her novels, 'Mr. Tallent's Ghost' is a light-hearted pastiche of a ghost story. It was published in Lady Cynthia Asquith's edited collection *The Ghost Book* in 1926.

T HE FIRST TIME I EVER MET MR. TALLENT WAS IN THE LATE
summer of 1906, in a small, lonely inn on the top of a mountain. For natives, rainy days in these places are not very different
from other days, since work fills them all, wet or fine. But for the
tourist, rainy days are boring. I had been bored for nearly a week,
and was thinking of returning to London, when Mr. Tallent came.
And because I could not "place" Mr. Tallent, nor elucidate him to
my satisfaction, he intrigued me. For a barrister should be able to
sum up men in a few minutes.

I did not see Mr. Tallent arrive, nor did I observe him entering the room. I looked up, and he was there, in the small firelit
parlour with its Bible, wool mats and copper preserving pan. He
was reading a manuscript, slightly moving his lips as he read. He
was a gentle, moth-like man, very lean and about six foot three or
more. He had neutral-coloured hair and eyes, a nondescript suit,
limp-looking hands and slightly turned-up toes. The most notice-
able thing about him was an expression of passive and enduring
obstinacy.

I wished him good evening, and asked if he had a paper, as he
seemed to have come from civilisation.

"No," he said softly, "no. Only a little manuscript of my own."

Now, as a rule I am as wary of manuscripts as a hare is of grey-
hounds. Having once been a critic, I am always liable to receive
parcels of these for advice. So I might have saved myself and a
dozen or so of other people from what turned out to be a terrible,
an appalling, incubus. But the day had been so dull, and having

exhausted Old Moore and sampled the Imprecatory Psalms, I had nothing else to read. So I said, "Your own?"

"Even so," replied Mr. Tallent modestly.

"May I have the privilege?" I queried, knowing he intended me to have it.

"How kind!" he exclaimed. "A stranger, knowing nothing of my hopes and aims, yet willing to undertake so onerous a task."

"Not at all!" I replied, with a nervous chuckle.

"I think," he murmured, drawing near and, as it were, taking possession of me, looming above me with his great height, "it might be best for me to read it to you. I am considered to have rather a fine reading voice."

I said I should be delighted, reflecting that supper could not very well be later than nine. I knew I should not like the reading.

He stood before the cloth-draped mantelpiece.

"This," he said, "shall be my rostrum." Then he read.

I wish I could describe to you that slow, expressionless, unstoppable voice. It was a voice for which at the time I could find no comparison. Now I know that it was like the voice of the loud speaker in a dull subject. At first one listened, taking in even the sense of the words. I took in all the first six chapters, which were unbelievably dull. I got all the scenery, characters, undramatic events clearly marshalled. I imagined that something would, in time, happen. I thought the characters were going to develop, do fearful things or great and holy deeds. But they did nothing. Nothing happened. The book was flat, formless, yet not vital enough to be inchoate. It was just a meandering expression of a negative personality, with a plethora of muted, borrowed, stale ideas. He always said what one expected him to say. One knew what all his people would do. One waited for the culminating platitude as for an expected twinge of toothache. I thought he would pause after a time, for even the most arrogant usually do that, apologising and at the same time obviously waiting for one to say, "Do go on, please."

This was not necessary in his case. In fact, it was impossible. The slow, monotonous voice went on without a pause, with the terrible tirelessness of a gramophone. I longed for him to whisper or shout—anything to relieve the tedium. I tried to think of other things, but he read too distinctly for that. I could neither listen to him nor ignore him. I have never spent such an evening. As luck would have it the little maidservant did not achieve our meal till nearly ten o'clock. The hours dragged on.

At last I said: "Could we have a pause, just for a few minutes?"

"Why?" he enquired.

"For… for discussion," I weakly murmured.

"Not," he replied, "at the most exciting moment. Don't you realise that now, at last, I have worked up my plot to the most dramatic moment? All the characters are waiting, attent, for the culminating tragedy."

He went on reading. I went on awaiting the culminating tragedy. But there was no tragedy. My head ached abominably. The voice flowed on, over my senses, the room, the world. I felt as if it would wash me away into eternity. I found myself thinking, quite solemnly:

"If she doesn't bring supper soon, I shall kill him."

I thought it in the instinctive way in which one thinks it of an earwig or a midge. I took refuge in the consideration how to do it? This was absorbing. It enabled me to detach myself completely from the sense of what he read. I considered all the ways open to me. Strangling. The bread knife on the sideboard. Hanging. I gloated over them, I was beginning to be almost happy, when suddenly the reading stopped.

"She is bringing supper," he said. "Now we can have a little discussion. Afterwards I will finish the manuscript."

He did. And after that, he told me all about his will. He said he was leaving all his money for the posthumous publication of his manuscripts. He also said that he would like me to draw up this for him, and to be trustee of the manuscripts.

I said I was too busy. He replied that I could draw up the will to-morrow.

"I'm going to-morrow," I interpolated passionately.

"You cannot go until the carrier goes in the afternoon," he triumphed. "Meanwhile, you can draw up the will. After that you need do no more. You can pay a critic to read the manuscripts. You can pay a publisher to publish them. And I in them shall be remembered."

He added that if I still had doubts as to their literary worth, he would read me another.

I gave in. Would anyone else have done differently? I drew up the will, left an address where he could send his stuff, and left the inn.

"Thank God!" I breathed devoutly, as the turn of the lane hid him from view. He was standing on the doorstep, beginning to read what he called a pastoral to a big cattle-dealer who had called for a pint of bitter. I smiled to think how much more he would get than he had bargained for.

After that, I forgot Mr. Tallent. I heard nothing more of him for some years. Occasionally I glanced down the lists of books to see if anybody else had relieved me of my task by publishing Mr. Tallent. But nobody had.

It was about ten years later, when I was in hospital with a "Blighty" wound, that I met Mr. Tallent again. I was convalescent, sitting in the sun with some other chaps, when the door opened softly, and Mr. Tallent stole in. He read to us for two hours. He remembered me, and had a good deal to say about coincidence. When he had gone, I said to the nurse, "If you let that fellow in again while I'm here, I'll kill him."

She laughed a good deal, but the other chaps all agreed with me, and as a matter of fact, he never did come again.

Not long after this I saw the notice of his death in the paper.

"Poor chap!" I thought, "he's been reading too much. Somebody's patience has given out. Well, he won't ever be able to read to me again."

Then I remembered the manuscripts, realising that, if he had been as good as his word, my troubles had only just begun.

And it was so.

First came the usual kind of letter from a solicitor in the town where he had lived. Next I had a call from the said solicitor's clerk, who brought a large tin box.

"The relations," he said, "of the deceased are extremely angry. Nothing has been left to them. They say that the manuscripts are worthless, and that the living have rights."

I asked how they knew that the manuscripts were worthless.

"It appears, sir, that Mr. Tallent has, from time to time, read these aloud—"

I managed to conceal a grin.

"And they claim, sir, to share equally with the—er—manuscripts. They threaten to take proceedings, and have been getting legal opinions as to the advisability of demanding an investigation of the material you have."

I looked at the box. There was an air of Joanna Southcott about it. I asked if it were full.

"Quite, sir. Typed MSS. Very neatly done."

He produced the key, a copy of the will, and a sealed letter.

I took the box home with me that evening. Fortified by dinner, a cigar and a glass of port, I considered it. There is an extraordinary air of fatality about a box. For bane or for blessing, it has a perpetual fascination for mankind. A wizard's coffer, a casket of jewels, the alabaster box of precious nard, a chest of bridal linen, a stone sarcophagus—what a strange mystery is about them all! So when I opened Mr. Tallent's box, I felt like somebody letting loose a genie. And indeed I was. I had already perused the will and the letter, and discovered that the fortune was moderately large. The letter merely repeated what Mr. Tallent had told me. I glanced at some of the manuscripts. Immediately the room seemed full of Mr. Tallent's presence and his voice. I looked towards the now dusky corners of the room as if he might be looming there. As I ran through more of the papers, I realised that what Mr. Tallent had chosen to read to me had been the best of them. I looked up Johnson's telephone number and asked him to come round. He is the kind of chap who never makes any money. He is a freelance journalist with a conscience. I knew he would be glad of the job.

He came round at once. He eyed the manuscripts with rapture. For at heart he is a critic, and has the eternal hope of unearthing a masterpiece.

"You had better take a dozen at a time, and keep a record," I said. "Verdict at the end."

"Will it depend on me whether they are published?"

"*Which* are published," I said. "Some will have to be. The will says so."

"But if I found them all worthless, the poor beggars would get more of the cash? Damnable to be without cash."

"I shall have to look into that. I am not sure if it is legally possible. What, for instance, is the standard?"

"I shall create the standard," said Johnson rather haughtily. "Of course, if I find a masterpiece—"

"If you find a masterpiece, my dear chap," I said, "I'll give you a hundred pounds."

He asked if I had thought of a publisher. I said I had decided on Jukes, since no book, however bad, could make his reputation worse than it was, and the money might save his credit.

"Is that quite fair to poor Tallent?" he asked. Mr. Tallent had already got hold of him.

"If," I said as a parting benediction, "you wish you had never gone into it (as, when you have put your hand to the plough, you will), remember that at least they were never read aloud to you, and be thankful."

Nothing occurred for a week. Then letters began to come from Mr. Tallent's relations. They were a prolific family. They were all very poor, very angry and intensely uninterested in literature. They wrote from all kinds of view-points, in all kinds of styles. They were, however, all alike in two things—the complete absence of literary excellence and legal exactitude.

It took an increasing time daily to read and answer these. If I gave them any hope, I at once felt Mr. Tallent's hovering presence, mute, anxious, hurt. If I gave no hope, I got a solicitor's letter by return of post. Nobody but myself seemed to feel the pathos of Mr. Tallent's ambitions and dreams. I was notified that proceedings were going to be taken by firms all over England. Money was being recklessly spent to rob Mr. Tallent of his immortality, but it appeared, later, that Mr. Tallent could take care of himself.

When Johnson came for more of the contents of the box, he said that there was no sign of a masterpiece yet, and that they were as bad as they well could be.

"A pathetic chap, Tallent," he said.

"Don't, for God's sake, my dear chap, let him get at you," I implored him. "Don't give way. He'll haunt you, as he's haunting me, with that abominable pathos of his. I think of him and his box continually just as one does of a life and death plea. If I sit by my own fireside, I can hear him reading. When I am just going to sleep, I dream that he is looming over me like an immense, wan moth. If I forget him for a little while, a letter comes from one of his unutterable relations and recalls me. Be wary of Tallent."

Needless to tell you that he did not take my advice. By the time he had finished the box, he was as much under Tallent's thumb as I was. Bitterly disappointed that there was no masterpiece, he was still loyal to the writer, yet he was emotionally harrowed by the pitiful letters that the relations were now sending to all the papers.

"I dreamed," he said to me one day (Johnson always says "dreamed", because he is a critic and considers it the elegant form of expression), "I dreamed that poor Tallent appeared to me in the watches of the night and told me exactly how each of his things came to him. He said they came like 'Kubla Khan'."

I said it must have taken all night.

"It did," he replied. "And it has made me dislike a masterpiece."

I asked him if he intended to be present at the general meeting.

"Meeting?"

"Yes. Things have got to such a pitch that we have had to call one. There will be about a hundred people. I shall have to entertain them to a meal afterwards. I can't very well charge it up to the account of the deceased."

"Gosh! It'll cost a pretty penny."

"It will. But perhaps we shall settle something. I shall be thankful."

"You're not looking well, old chap," he said, "Worn, you seem."

"I am," I said. "Tallent is ever with me. Will you come?"

"Rather. But I don't know what to say."

"The truth, the whole truth—"

"But it's so awful to think of that poor soul spending his whole life on those damned... and then that they should never see the light of day."

"Worse that they should. Much worse."

"My dear chap, what a confounded position!"

"If I had foreseen *how* confounded," I said, "I'd have strangled the fellow on the top of that mountain. I have had to get two clerks to deal with the correspondence. I get no rest. All night I dream of Tallent. And now I hear that a consumptive relation of his has died of disappointment at not getting any of the money, and his wife has written me a wild letter threatening to accuse me of manslaughter. Of course that's all stuff, but it shows what a hysterical state everybody's in. I feel pretty well done for."

"You'd feel worse if you'd read the boxful."

I agreed.

We had a stormy meeting. It was obvious that the people did need the money. They were the sort of struggling, under-vitalised folk who always do need it. Children were waiting for a chance in life, old people were waiting to be saved from death a little longer, middle-aged people were waiting to set themselves up in business or buy snug little houses. And there was Tallent, out of it all, in a spiritual existence, not needing beef and bread any more, deliberately keeping it from them.

As I thought this, I distinctly saw Tallent pass the window of the room I had hired for the occasion. I stood up; I pointed; I cried out to them to follow him. The very man himself.

Johnson came to me.

"Steady, old man," he said. "You're overstrained."

"But I did see him," I said. "The very man. The cause of all the mischief. If I could only get my hands on him!"

A medical man who had married one of Tallent's sisters said that these hallucinations were very common, and that I was evidently not a fit person to have charge of the money. This brought me a ray of hope, till that ass Johnson contradicted him, saying foolish things about my career. And a diversion was caused by a tremulous old lady calling out, "The Church! The Church! Consult the Church! There's something in the Bible about it, only I can't call it to mind at the moment. Has anybody got a Bible?"

A clerical nephew produced a pocket New Testament, and it transpired that what she had meant was, "Take ten talents."

"If I could take one, madam," I said, "it would be enough."

"It speaks of that too," she replied triumphantly. "Listen! 'If any man have one talent...' Oh, there's everything in the Bible!"

"Let us," remarked one of the thirteen solicitors, "get to business. Whether it's in the Bible or not, whether Mr. Tallent went past the window or not, the legality or illegality of what we propose is not affected. Facts are facts. The deceased is dead. *You've* got the money. *We* want it."

"I devoutly wish you'd got it," I said, "and that Tallent was haunting you instead of me."

The meeting lasted four hours. The wildest ideas were put forward. One or two sporting cousins of the deceased suggested a decision by games—representatives of the would-be beneficiaries and representatives of the manuscript. They were unable to see that this could not affect the legal aspect. Johnson was asked for his opinion. He said that from a critic's point of view the MSS. were balderdash. Everybody looked kindly upon him. But just as he was sunning himself in this atmosphere, and trying to forget Tallent, an immense lady, like Boadicea, advanced upon him, towering over him in a hostile manner.

"I haven't read the books, and I'm not going to," she said, "but I take exception to that word balderdash, sir, and I consider it libellous. Let me tell you, I brought Mr. Tallent into the world!" I looked at her with awesome wonder. She had brought that portent into the world! But how... whom had she persuaded?... I pulled myself up. And as I turned away from the contemplation of Boadicea, I saw Tallent pass the window again.

I rushed forward and tried to push up the sash. But the place was built for meetings, not for humanity, and it would not open. I seized the poker, intending to smash the glass. I suppose I must have looked rather mad, and as everybody else had been too intent on business to look out of the window, nobody believed that I had seen anything.

"You might just go round to the nearest chemist's and get some bromide," said the doctor to Johnson. "He's over-wrought."

Johnson, who was thankful to escape Boadicea, went with alacrity.

The meeting was, however, over at last. A resolution was passed that we should try to arrange things out of court. We were to take the opinions of six eminent lawyers—judges preferably. We were also to submit what Johnson thought the best story to a distinguished critic. According to what they said we were to divide the money up or leave things as they were.

I felt very much discouraged as I walked home. All these opinions would entail much work and expense. There seemed no end to it.

"Damn the man!" I muttered, as I turned the corner into the square in which I live. And there, just the width of the square away from me, was the man himself. I could almost have wept. What had I done that the gods should play with me thus?

I hurried forward, but he was walking fast, and in a moment he turned down a side-street. When I got to the corner, the street was empty. After this, hardly a day passed without my seeing Tallent. It made me horribly jumpy and nervous, and the fear of madness began to prey on my mind. Meanwhile, the business went on. It was finally decided that half the money should be divided among the relations. Now I thought there would be peace, and for a time there was—comparatively.

But it was only about a month from this date that I heard from one of the solicitors to say that a strange and disquieting thing had happened—two of the beneficiaries were haunted by Mr. Tallent to such an extent that their reason was in danger. I wrote to ask what form the haunting took. He said they continually heard Mr. Tallent reading aloud from his works. Wherever they were in the house, they still heard him. I wondered if he would begin reading to me soon. So far it had only been visions. If he began to read...

In a few months I heard that both the relations who were haunted had been taken to an asylum. While they were in the asylum they heard nothing. But, some time after, on being certified as cured and released, they heard the reading again, and had to go back. Gradually the same thing happened to others, but only to one or two at a time.

During the long winter, two years after his death, it began to happen to me.

I immediately went to a specialist, who said there was acute nervous prostration, and recommended a "home". But I refused. I would fight Tallent to the last. Six of the beneficiaries were now in "homes", and every penny of the money they had had was used up.

I considered things. "Bell, book and candle" seemed to be what was required. But how, when, where to find him? I consulted a spiritualist, a priest and a woman who has more intuitive perception than anyone I know. From their advice I made my plans. But it was Lesbia who saved me.

"Get a man who can run to go about with you," she said. "The moment *He* appears, let your companion rush round by a side-street and cut him off."

"But how will that—?"

"Never mind. I know what I think."

She gave me a wise little smile.

I did what she advised, but it was not till my patience was nearly exhausted that I saw Tallent again. The reading went on, but only in the evenings when I was alone, and at night. I asked people in evening after evening. But when I got into bed, it began.

Johnson suggested that I should get married.

"What?" I said, "offer a woman a ruined nervous system, a threatened home, and a possible end in an asylum?"

"There's one woman who would jump at it. I love my love with an L."

"Don't be an ass," I said. I felt in no mood for jokes. All I wanted was to get things cleared up.

About three years after Tallent's death, my companion and I, going out rather earlier than usual, saw him hastening down a long road which had no side-streets leading out of it. As luck would have it, an empty taxi passed us. I shouted. We got in. Just in front of Tallent's ghost we stopped, leapt out, and flung ourselves upon him.

"My God!" I cried. "He's *solid!*"

He was perfectly solid, and not a little alarmed.

We put him into the taxi and took him to my house.

"*Now,* Tallent!" I said, "you will answer for what you have done."

He looked scared, but dreamy.

"Why aren't you dead?" was my next question.

He seemed hurt.

"I never died," he replied softly.

"It was in the papers."

"I put it in. I was in America. It was quite easy."

"And that continual haunting of me, and the wicked driving of your unfortunate relations into asylums?" I was working myself into a rage. "Do you know how many of them are there now?"

"Yes. I know. Very interesting."

"Interesting?"

"It was in a great cause," he said. "Possibly you didn't grasp that I was a progressive psycho-analyst, and that I did not take those novels of mine seriously. In fact, they were just part of the experiment."

"In heaven's name, *what* experiment?"

"The plural would be better, really," he said, "for there were many experiments."

"But what for, you damned old blackguard?" I shouted.

"For my *magnum opus,*" he said modestly.

"And what is your abominable *magnum opus,* you wicked old man?"

"It will be famous all over the world," he said complacently. "All this has given me exceptional opportunities. It was so easy to get into my relations' houses and experiment with them. It was regrettable, though, that I could not follow them to the asylum."

This evidently worried him far more than the trouble he had caused.

"So it was *you* reading, every time?"

"Every time."

"And it was you who went past the window of that horrible room when we discussed your will?"

"Yes. A most gratifying spectacle!"

"And now, you old scoundrel, before I decide what to do with you," I said, "what is the *magnum opus*?"

"It is a treatise," he said, with the pleased expression that made me so wild. "A treatise that will eclipse all former work in that field, and its title is—'An Exhaustive Enquiry, with numerous Experiments, into the Power of Human Endurance'."

THE LOST TRAGEDY (1926)

Denis Mackail (1892–1971)

Grandson of Edward Burne-Jones and brother of the more famous novelist Angela Thirkell, Denis Mackail worked in varied jobs—theatrical roles, including set design and stage management; then, after the outbreak of the First World War, in the War Office, the Board of Trade, and the Print Room at the British Museum. He started writing novels as a way of earning an additional income to help support his wife and two children, and was prolific until the death of his wife in 1949. Today his works are almost forgotten, with the exception of the novel *Greenery Street* (1925), which was republished by Persephone Books in 2002.

This amusing and very 1920s story explores what happens when a mysterious person will stop at nothing to prevent the rediscovery of a less-than-classic book.

M R. BUNSTABLE'S BOOK-SHOP REPRESENTS A TYPE OF ESTAB-
lishment which has pretty well disappeared from our
modern cities. Indeed, but for the fear of becoming involved in
correspondence with strangers, I should be prepared to go considerably further, and to say that it is the only shop of its kind still
in existence. In any case, it is most distinctly and unmistakably a
survival from the past.

As all who have considered the subject must agree, the principal object of any bookseller is to obstruct, as far as possible, the
sale of books. The method generally adopted to-day is to fill the
premises with intelligent young men with knobby foreheads who
chase intending customers from shelf to shelf, thrusting novels at
antiquarians, theological works at novel-readers, and two-volume
biographies at those who obviously cannot afford them, until
finally they have chased their victims right out into the street. This
is called scientific salesmanship, and is largely responsible for the
profits shown by the circulating libraries.

The old-fashioned method was directed at the same end, but by
a totally different route. The intending customer was left utterly
and entirely to himself. If he knew what he wanted to read, he
read it without let or hindrance and equally without payment.
If he were just vaguely in search of an unidentified book—let us
suppose for a wedding present—then he would wait for a period
which varied according to his patience and temperament, and
ultimately would take his departure and buy a silver sauce-boat
elsewhere.

Mr. Bunstable was, and still is, a skilled exponent of this second and earlier form of book-selling. He does not go in for window-dressing, and the wares which are visible from the street seem to have been chosen principally for their power to exclude the daylight from the interior of his shop, and secondarily for a lack of interest which shall ensure their remaining undisturbed. If you persist in disregarding the warning of this window, your next difficulty is with the door. Owing to a slight settlement in the fabric of Mr. Bunstable's premises it is impossible to open this door without the exercise of both strength and skill, but if you do succeed in opening it, then beware of the step which lurks just inside. Inexperienced customers usually arrive in the shop with a crash and a cry of alarm, and perhaps it is because of this that Mr. Bunstable has never troubled to repair the bell which hangs over his lintel, and was originally intended to give notice of his clients' approach.

As your eyes become accustomed to the darkness within, you now detect one or more figures, standing more or less erect with their legs more or less twisted round each other, and profoundly absorbed in the books which they are reading. Here again, and before they have discovered that these figures are wearing hats, inexperienced customers have mistaken them for members of Mr. Bunstable's staff. But no contretemps has ever arisen from this misapprehension. The figures are so intent on their studies that they are deaf to any words which may be addressed to them, and the customer can retrieve his error without any spoken explanation. One imagines that towards closing-time Mr. Bunstable must go round his shop removing the volumes from these students' hands, and gently pushing them back into the outer world. But it is almost as easy to suppose that some of them remain there all night, for so far as my own observation goes Mr. Bunstable regards them as part of the fittings and fixtures. One day I must really go there at closing-time and see what happens.

Meanwhile your eyes are becoming more and more acclimatised. You see vistas and vistas of books. Books heaped up on the dusty floor; books rising in tiers to the mottled ceiling; books on tables; books piled precariously on a step-ladder; books bursting out of brown-paper parcels; books balanced on the seats of chairs. You long to *sneeze*—for the violence of your entrance has sent a quantity of dust flying up your nose—but you control yourself heroically. The atmosphere of the place would make such an action an outrage. It would be worse than sneezing in church.

It was at this stage, in my own case, and just as I was wondering how on earth one ever bought anything in this extraordinary shop, that another of my senses was unexpectedly assailed. Somewhere—for the moment I couldn't tell where—a tune was being whistled. A short, monotonous air which suggested "Here we go round the mulberry bush", and other works of that nature, and yet refused to be identified as anything that I had heard before. I looked at the two drugged readers who were the only other visible occupants of the shop, but the sound wasn't coming from them. Nor, on the other hand, did they give any sign of interest or annoyance at the constant repetition of that little tune.

You will sympathise, I hope, when I say that it had now become my most pressing requirement to track the whistler to his lair; and with this object in view I penetrated still farther into the darkness of the shop, stepping over the heaps of books and the brown-paper parcels, and soon losing all sense of direction in a labyrinth of shelves. All this while the tune continued, but as I felt my way forward I noticed another peculiarity about it. The whistler seemed to have some rooted objection to giving us the last note of his melody. Each time that he reached this point, and each time that I was convinced the key-note must be coming, he suddenly broke off, paused for a moment, and began again at the beginning. It was all that I could do not to supply the missing note myself. And yet if, as I was now coming to believe, the music were proceeding from the proprietor of the shop, this was hardly the conventional way of introducing myself to his notice.

Again I controlled myself, and then suddenly—as I turned yet another corner—I beheld the explanation of my puzzle. I was at the door of an inner sanctum or den, bursting with books also, yet differing from the dusty profusion through which I had come in that they were all neatly and carefully arranged; and between me and the window, which opened on to a prospect of unrelieved brickwork, there hung a small bird-cage.

"Oh," I exclaimed aloud. "A bullfinch."

At the same moment a second, and human, silhouette appeared before the window. Afterwards I saw that it had risen from a large desk, but at the time it had the startling effect of emerging as from a trap-door, and what with this and my embarrassment at having been overheard, I took a hasty step backward.

"Don't go, sir," said the silhouette. "Was there anything I could find for you?"

It was in this way that I first met Mr. Edward Bunstable, the sole proprietor of the shop which I have attempted to describe, and the individual to whom I owe the story that I am trying to relate. He was, and still is, a shortish gentleman of a genial but moderate rotundity, the possessor of a beard and a pair of steel-rimmed spectacles. He knows more about out-of-the-way books than anyone I have ever met, and how in the world he keeps his trade going and pays rent, rates and taxes out of it, it is impossible to guess. I have enjoyed the privilege of his acquaintanceship for a number of years now, but though he has frequently shown me volumes which he has bought, I have never yet been able to discover any volume which he has sold. Sometimes I think that he must be an eccentric millionaire—so utterly unbusinesslike are his ways of business; at other times I am fain to believe that he is some kind of fairy, or ghost, or magician, or that he has escaped from the pages of one of his mustiest volumes—but I think this is because secretly he rather enjoys mystifying me. There has been a hint of a twinkle from behind those steel-rimmed spectacles during some of our talks which seems to me to support this view.

I have no idea where he sleeps, when he eats, or what—within about forty years—his age may be. On the other hand I know all these particulars about his bullfinch, for within three minutes of our first meeting—and while I was still trying to give him the name of the book that I wanted—he had told me that the bullfinch never left his room, that it subsisted on millet seed, and that it was fifteen years old. "I bought him cheap," he said, "because he never could learn the last note of his song. I spent ten years trying to teach it him, but it was no use. That bird's got *character*, he has."

"Oh yes," I said. "But about this book, I was wondering if—"

"That bird," interrupted Mr. Bunstable, "is a regular Londoner. He's as sharp as they're made, that bird is."

He told me a great deal more about his bullfinch's alleged characteristics before I could succeed in giving him the particulars of the book that I was after. Then he nodded his head with an air of infinite wisdom.

"I've got it," he said. "I can't just lay my hands on it at the moment, but if you were to come back—say in two or three days' time…"

Knowing no better, I did as I was asked. Mr. Bunstable said that he was still searching for the book. He was more convinced than ever that it was somewhere on the premises, but his general attitude towards the affair was that it was no use hurrying things. The suggestion conveyed to me at the time was that if once the book became aware that he was looking for it, it might take fright and disappear for good. After telling me a number of anecdotes of a literary flavour and showing me several of his most recent purchases—which he was careful to explain were not to be included in his stock—he proposed that I should pay him another visit, say in about a week or ten days.

"I'll be certain to have it for you by then," he added. "I *know* I've got it put away somewhere."

To cut a long story short, the object of my original enquiry has eluded Mr. Bunstable's search to this day. He is still hopeful about it, though I have long since abandoned any expectation of its ever coming to light—just as I have long since outgrown the whim which made me ask for it. If he should ever find it, of course I would offer to buy it. This would at least be due to a man who, at a very moderate reckoning, has spent about a fortnight of working days in trying to oblige a customer. I shall not be surprised, however, if—in the event of its turning up—Mr. Bunstable refuses to part with it. For in the meantime there have been one or two near shaves when I have tried to purchase other volumes from his collection, and each time he has managed to prevent the sale taking place.

"Don't take it now, sir," he has said. "I'll find a better copy if you'll wait." Or, "I wouldn't have it, if I were you, sir. There'll be a new edition out in the spring." If I am still persistent, he enmeshes me in one of his long and hypnotic anecdotes, edging me quietly towards the door as he tells it. By this means I am caused to forget

the quest which had drawn me to his shop, and his honour as an
old-fashioned bookseller is preserved.

An inexplicable old gentleman. Even now, as I set this description on paper, I find myself wondering whether he and his shop
can really exist. And perhaps this uncertainty is one of the reasons
why I keep on going back there. I want to convince myself that I
haven't made it all up.

So we arrive at the story which Mr. Bunstable told me one evening last autumn—beginning it in the recesses of his inner sanctum,
with the bullfinch contributing its familiar *obbligato,* and finishing
it at the front door of his shop, as he bowed me out into the foggy
street. A good title for it might be "The Lost Tragedy".

Personally (said Mr. Bunstable) I'm a great one for reading, and
perhaps you'll say that's natural enough. But there've been some
big men in my trade—men who are up to all the tricks of the
auction-room—who'd buy and sell books by the thousand, and
yet never read anything but a catalogue or a newspaper, or maybe
a railway time-table. Not that they weren't fond of books. But it
was the bindings they cared for, or the leaves being uncut, or the
first edition with all the misprints and the suppressed preface—*you*
know, sir; the things that run up the value of a book without any
reference to what that book's about. Of course, we've all got to
watch out for these details, but to my mind—when all's said and
done—a book's a thing to read. You can't get away from *that*, sir.

But the man I learnt the business from—old Mr. Trumpett—I
was twenty years in his shop in Panton Street before I set up on my
own—*he* wouldn't have agreed with me. Not he, sir. He'd got an
eye for rarities which was worth a fortune; he'd got a collection of
old editions which was worth another fortune; and he could run

rings round anyone in the sale-room. But he didn't worry about what was inside a book. Not he. Many a time he's hauled me over the coals for sitting reading in his shop. "You stick to the title-pages, my boy," he's said. "That's all a bookseller needs to know about." And I'll say this for Mr. Trumpett, he certainly practised what he preached.

He used to travel about a good deal, attending sales outside London or helping in valuations for probate where there was a big library; and sometimes—though not as often as I'd have liked—he'd take me along with him. It was a wonder to me the way he'd go into a room full of books in an old country house—all arranged anyhow and with no catalogue or anything to help him—and yet he'd pick out all the plums within five or ten minutes of getting there. It was almost as if he could *smell* 'em out, sir. Uncanny, you'd have called it, if you'd seen him on the job. Partly for practice and partly to amuse myself I'd try sometimes if I couldn't find something valuable that he'd missed; but I can't say that I ever succeeded. The nearest I ever came to it was with this book that I'm telling you about.

We'd gone down to a big country house where the owner had died, to see if we could pick anything up. The young fellow who'd come into the property was all for selling everything that he could, but when it came to the library the whole place was in such a mess that no one could trouble to make a proper inventory. The auctioneer's instructions were to sell the old books off in bundles as they stood on the shelves; and seeing the quantity of litter there was, I can't say it was a bad idea. The bindings had been pretty good in their day, though that had been some time ago, but as for the stuff inside—well, it was just the typical sermons and county histories and so forth that you could buy up anywhere. A regular lot of rubbish.

We got down there the morning of the day when that part of the sale was coming on, and old Mr. Trumpett didn't take long to size it all up. He marked down a few bundles which might about cover our railway fares, if he got them at a proper price, and then he was just thinking about getting some lunch when I pointed out to him that there was a shelf over one of the doors that we hadn't looked at.

"Nonsense," he said, for he didn't like admitting he could have missed anything. "I saw them when I first came in."

Of course we both knew quite well that he'd done nothing of the sort, but it wasn't going to pay me to get into an argument with him, so I just made up my mind that I'd come back after he'd gone and have a glance at those books myself. "Perhaps I'll get a chance," I thought, "to show him I'm not so ignorant as he thinks."

So just as we were going out of the front door, I pretended I'd left my pencil-case in the library and I went back there alone. To my surprise—for I hadn't been gone more than a minute and we certainly hadn't met anyone on the way—there was a gentleman standing on a chair with his back to me, reaching up at that particular shelf over the inner door. He'd got a cloak on—rather like people used to wear in Scotland—and as I could see a pair of rough stockings underneath it, I made up my mind he was a golfer. He was running through the books very quick and anxious-like, but he must have heard my step, for he stopped suddenly and turned round on his chair. He was rather a short gentleman, and a bit pale; rather thin on the top, if you know what I mean, and with a little pointed beard. It struck me that I'd seen him somewhere before, or else his photograph, but I couldn't put a name to him at the time, and of course—well, I'll come to that later.

He was looking at me so curiously that I felt I had to say something, so I thought I'd better explain what I'd come back for.

"When you've finished, sir," I said, "I wanted to have a look through that shelf for myself." And as he didn't answer, though I was certain he'd heard me quite clearly, I added: "I've come down from London for the sale."

He nodded very gravely and politely, and turned back to the book-shelf. He kept on taking out one volume after another and shoving them back again as soon as he'd looked inside. Then all of a sudden he gave a little gasp, and I saw him staring at an old quarto, bound in calf, that he'd just opened. The next moment he'd popped it under his cloak and jumped off the chair.

Well, I'd seen some pretty cool customers in the book trade before now, but this seemed to me to be a bit *too* cool.

"Here," I called out, backing between him and the doorway. "What are you doing with that book? You can't take it away like that."

"Can't I?" he said—and it seemed to me that he spoke like some kind of West-countryman. "It's mine."

"But you're not Mr. Hatteras, are you?" I asked—naming the heir to the property. For, you see, this gentleman was about fifty, I should judge.

"No," he said. "But the book is mine. If I choose to take it with me, what is that to you? It should never have been printed."

Well, sir, at that last remark of his I'll admit that I thought he was a little bit—well, *you* know what I mean. (Here Mr. Bunstable tapped his forehead expressively.) But that didn't seem to me any reason why he should make off with something that wasn't his.

"Look here, sir," I said, "I don't want to make any trouble, but I saw you putting a book from that shelf under your cloak, and unless you put it back where it came from I shall have to tell the auctioneer."

"The auctioneer?" he repeated, looking a bit puzzled.

"Yes," I said. "If you want any book out of this room, you can bid for it at the sale this afternoon." And as he still looked kind of silly, I pointed to the card that had been pinned over the shelf. "Lot 56," I said. "If you want that book, the proper way to get it is to bid for Lot 56."

For a moment I thought he was going to make a dash past me, but I wasn't surprised when he changed his mind, for he was a very nervous-looking gentleman, and he wouldn't have stood much chance if I'd wanted to stop him.

"So be it," he said, and he climbed on to the chair again and put the book back where he'd found it. Then with a funny sort of look at me, he went straight out of the room. "I wonder where I've seen that face before," I kept on thinking—but still I couldn't put a name to it.

Well, sir, by this time I saw that if I was going to get any lunch I should have to run for it, and as I was a young man in those days I decided to leave that last book-shelf and try to slip in again before the sale started. As I was going out through the hall, I ran into the auctioneer's clerk, and I thought it mightn't be a bad thing if I told him what I'd seen.

"All right," he said, when I'd finished. "I'll lock the library door, if there's anything of that sort going on. But did you say the gentleman had come out just now?"

"Yes," I said. "Just about a minute before I did."

"That's funny," he answered. "I was in the hall here the whole time, and I could have sworn nobody came by."

Well, it *was* funny, if you see what I mean, sir; and we both laughed a good deal at the time.

"Though apart from the principle of the thing," I said, "there's precious few books in there that are worth more than sixpence."

"That's as it may be," said the clerk cautiously. And I left him, and hurried off to the inn.

When I told Mr. Trumpett, he said, "H'm. That sounds like Badger of Liverpool. He'll get shut up one of these days if he's not careful." And he pulled out his copy of the sale catalogue and made a pencil mark against Lot 56. "He's a cunning old bird," he added. "If there's anything I've missed, we'll give him a run for his money."

And we did. I had no opportunity of seeing that shelf again, for the library was still locked when I got back, and the sale was to take place in the dining-room. But there was Mr. Badger of Liverpool, in his cloak and his golf-stockings, watching each lot as it came up and was knocked down, and when we got to Lot 56 he started bidding like a good 'un.

Mr. Trumpett sat there nodding his head to the auctioneer—for everyone but these two had soon dropped out—but when the price for the odd *dozen* books had run up to a hundred and twenty-five pounds, I suppose he felt he'd gone far enough for a pig in a poke. He closed his eyes and shook his head, in the way he had when he'd finished bidding, and the auctioneer brought his hammer down with a thump.

Of course I thought we'd heard the last of Lot 56, but just as I was crossing it off my list I heard the auctioneer having some kind of an argument with the successful bidder.

"These are no good to me," he was saying, holding out a handful of coins. "I can't take foreign money for my deposit."

Mr. Badger was a very nervous-looking gentleman, as I think I've told you, and he didn't seem to know what to make of this. He kept on snapping his fingers and starting sentences that he couldn't finish, but it was no use. The auctioneer simply dropped the money on his desk for Mr. Badger to take or leave as he chose, and announced that he was putting the lot up again. The little mystery and excitement that there'd been sent it up to seven-pound-ten, but at that figure the competition stopped and Mr. Trumpett got what he'd wanted. I could see the auctioneer looking pretty sick, but he was quite right, of course. Whatever those coins were, they'd have been no good to his employers. Why, some of them were scarcely even round!

Well, sir, we stopped on and picked up one or two more lots, and when we'd arranged for having them sent up to London we took a fly back to the station and caught our train. In the carriage I suddenly remembered rather a curious thing, and I mentioned it to Mr. Trumpett.

"Did you see where Mr. Badger went to?" I asked. "I never saw him leaving the room, but he wasn't there when we came away; that I'll swear."

Mr. Trumpett looked at me quite queer-like.

"Badger?" he repeated. "What do you mean?"

"Why," I said, "the gentleman who bid against you, sir, for Lot 56."

"That wasn't Badger," he says.

"Then who was it?" says I.

But Mr. Trumpett had no idea.

"I feel as if I'd seen his face somewhere," he said presently; "or else he's very like someone I've met. But I'm bothered if I can place him."

"If you ask me," he said, a little later on, "he'd broken loose from somewhere. Did you see the way his eyes were rolling?"

"Yes," I said. "Quite a fine frenzy, wasn't it?"

But of course my little literary allusion was wasted on Mr. Trumpett. He only grunted, and we dropped the subject for good.

Well (resumed Mr. Bunstable, who had now got me out of his labyrinth into the main part of the shop), a few days after that the packing-case came along from the sale, and though Mr. Trumpett would likely enough have let it lie in his cellar for weeks—for he took his time over most things—I thought I'd go down and look through the stuff myself. You see, I'd still got it in the back of my head that our golfing friend might have known a bit more than we'd given him credit for; that there really might be some sort of "find" in Lot 56. And if there was, then I meant to get to the bottom of it.

So late that afternoon I took a candle down to the cellar—we'd no gas except in the shop itself in those days—and I got a tack-lifter and a hammer, and started opening the case. Out it all came—most of it just about fit for a barrow in the street, though every now and then I'd find one of the books that Mr. Trumpett had spotted—and presently I'd got right down to the straw. And there—the last book to come out—was the calf-bound quarto that the gentleman in the cloak had tried to make away with. The label had come off the back and the leaves were still uncut, but when I turned to the title-page— well, I tell you, sir, I thought for a moment I must be dreaming.

What would *you* say, sir, I wonder, if you picked up an old book and found it was a play by Shakespeare that no one had ever imagined as existing ? Would you believe your eyes ? I tell you, I could hardly believe mine. Yet there it was—paper, type and binding all above suspicion, as I knew well enough—and on the title-page *The Tragedie of Alexander the Great, by Mr. William Shakespeare.* I felt like Christopher Columbus and Marconi rolled into one. The biggest discovery of the century, and I—down there by myself in Mr. Trumpett's cellar—had made it. I sat down on the edge of that packing-case and fairly gasped for breath. It was the most tremendous moment in my life.

Of course I knew it was my real duty to rush up the ladder into the shop and tell Mr. Trumpett what I'd found, and, of course, I meant to do this as soon as I'd collected my wits. But while I sat there staring at that title-page, I realised more and more clearly what Mr. Trumpett would do. The book would go straight into his safe—uncut as it was, so as to keep up the value; when it left the safe it would be to go direct to the saleroom, and from there—unless an Act of Parliament stopped it—to an American collector. If I carried out my duty without a thought of the consequences, my first opportunity of reading the *Tragedie of Alexander the Great* would be in a facsimile or reprint, just as if the original had never been in my hands at all. And I wanted to read it *now*. I was enough of a bookseller to recognise its enormous value, but—unlike Mr. Trumpett—I was too much of a book-lover to let that American collector read it first.

I wasn't going to cut the leaves, of course. I knew better than to do that. But there were pretty wide margins, and by twisting the pages carefully I could manage well enough; and so—sitting down on the packing-case and by the light of my candle—I began right away. *"Act I, Scene 1. A Room in King Philip's Palace."* Yes, sir; I remember that. But I'm thankful that I can't remember any more.

Did I say "thankful"? Well, sir, I'm afraid I mean it. I don't pretend to be a poet myself and in the ordinary way I'll admit there may be better critics. But when it comes to a real piece of downright incompetent, careless writing, of bad scansion and worse grammar, of loud-sounding, pretentious and meaningless clap-trap—then I'll take leave to say that I'm as good a judge as most men. It was awful, sir; it was terrible. It was like a parody of the worst kind of Elizabethan poetry, and yet, if you see what I mean, it *was* Elizabethan poetry. Not a word, not a phrase to give the show away—as there are in Chatterton's forgeries. It was like Shakespeare read through some kind of distorting lens, with all the faults and weaknesses—for he *had* faults and weaknesses, sir—magnified ten thousand times, and all the beauty cancelled right out.

"No wonder they kept this out of the First Folio," I kept on telling myself. And yet I couldn't put it down. However bad it might be, it *was*—unless some contemporary had played an expensive practical joke—the discovery that I had taken it for. And I was the first of my own contemporaries to read it. In spite of myself, though, my excitement had given way to an almost overwhelming sense of depression. If you're really fond of books, sir, that's always the way a piece of thoroughly bad workmanship takes you.

I don't know how long I'd been down in that cellar (resumed Mr. Bunstable, after a short and mournful pause), when all of a sudden I heard a kind of thud overhead; and looking up I saw that someone had closed the trap at the top of the ladder. "Good heavens," I thought, "there's Mr. Trumpett going off for the night, and if I don't hurry after him I shall be locked in." I jumped up, picked up my candle and was just moving to the foot of the ladder, when to my astonishment I saw that two men were standing in my way. It seemed to me that they were in some kind of fancy dress, and what with this and my bewilderment at the way they'd managed to get in, I very nearly dropped the candle. Then, as I recovered it, I recognised the shorter of them. It was the old gentleman that I'd seen last week at that sale down in the country; the gentleman that I'd taken for Mr. Badger of Liverpool.

"What's the matter?" I asked in a shaking kind of voice. "What do you want, sir?"

He didn't answer me, but turned to his companion—a big, burly sort of fellow, who struck me as knowing pretty well what the bottom of a pint-pot looked like.

"Did you bolt the trap, Ben?" he asked. "Are you sure the old man's gone?"

"What do you take me for?" said the big fellow, speaking with a kind of rough, Cockney accent. "Of course he's gone. Now, then," he added, looking at me, "we've come for that book. Where have you put it?"

I had it under my arm, but before I could answer him he'd spotted it.

"Aha!" he called out. "There you are, Will. What did I tell you? Didn't I say we'd find it here?"

They both seemed tremendously excited, and I was convinced that they'd been drinking; but I wasn't going to stand any nonsense.

"I don't know what you're doing here," I said, retreating behind the packing-case, "or how you've forced your way in. But this book has been bought and paid for by my employer, Mr. Trumpett, and let me remind you that you've no right in the private part of the shop."

The big man only laughed at this, but the other started talking sixteen to the dozen.

"And let me tell *you*," he said, "that that book was published without any authority, that the script was stolen from the theatre and that anyone who keeps it is a receiver of stolen goods. Do you know what I spent in buying up that edition from the blackguard who printed it ? Two hundred angels. And do you know how long I've been hunting for the copy he kept back ? Nearly three hundred years! But I've found it at last, and I'm going to see that it's destroyed. I've got my reputation to protect the same as anyone else, and if I did a bit of pot-boiling because I'd got into debt that's no reason why it should be brought up against me now. I've had enough trouble over *Pericles* and *Titus Andronicus,* without being saddled with a bit of balderdash like *Alexander the Great.* You got the better of me down in Gloucestershire last week, but it's my turn now. I've got good friends, I have, who'll see that justice is done. If I'm a bit scant of breath myself, here's my old colleague Jonson, who's killed his man more than once and will do it again for the honour of the profession. Now, then, young sir, are you going to hand that play over, or do you want a taste of Ben's dagger in your gullet?"

That's the way he ran on, sir, though I may not have got all his words quite right, and all the time the other man was rocking and shaking with laughter. I was so scared I could hardly think, for it was no joke being shut up down there with two fellows like that. Mad, they might be, or drunk, or both together; but whatever they were, I could see they would stick at nothing. And yet...

Well, sir, it's no use reproaching myself now. And, besides, after all these years I'm not at all sure that the actual upshot wasn't the best for everybody. The big fellow had jumped right over the packing-case and twisted my arms together behind my back, while the little one snatched the book from where it had fallen, tore out the sheets and burnt them one by one in the flame of my candle. Then he threw the empty binding down on the cellar floor.

"All's well that ends well," he said, "He's had his lesson, Ben. You can let him go."

And then he stooped down and blew out the candle.

As he reached this stage in his remarkable narrative, Mr. Bunstable stretched past me with one hand and opened the door of his shop. A cold draught accompanied by wisps of London fog blew in through the aperture, causing me to shiver and Mr. Bunstable to utter his little, dry, grating cough. Far away I heard the indomitable bullfinch once more embarking on his incomplete melody. The rest was silence.

"You mean," I said presently, "that it was a dream?"

"Eh?" said Mr. Bunstable, starting from his thoughts. "Well, sir, as to that I should hardly like to say. I certainly spent the night in that cellar, as Mr. Trumpett could tell you if he were alive. And I'll have to admit that there were no traces of that book on the floor—no ashes, even—when I looked for them in the morning. And yet that doesn't seem to me to explain everything. Because, sir, there was no calf-bound quarto there either. You've only got my word for it, of course, but…"

And here, gently but firmly, Mr. Bunstable shut me out into the fog.

THE BOOK (1930)

Margaret Irwin (1889–1967)

Margaret Emma Faith Irwin is probably best known as an historical novelist focusing mainly on the Elizabethan and Stuart periods, but she also wrote a large number of short stories mostly for publication in *The London Mercury*. This story on a Faustian theme appeared in the September 1930 edition, and was later republished in Irwin's collection of supernatural tales, *Madame Fears the Dark* (1935). It has frequently been anthologised since, with good reason.

O N A FOGGY NIGHT IN NOVEMBER, MR. CORBETT, HAVING guessed the murderer by the third chapter of his detective story, arose in disappointment from his bed and went downstairs in search of something more satisfactory to send him to sleep.

The fog had crept through the closed and curtained windows of the dining-room and hung thick on the air in a silence that seemed as heavy and breathless as the fog. The atmosphere was more choking than in his room, and very chill, although the remains of a large fire still burned in the grate.

The dining-room bookcase was the only considerable one in the house and held a careless unselected collection to suit all the tastes of the household, together with a few dull and obscure old theological books that had been left over from the sale of a learned uncle's library. Cheap red novels, bought on railway stalls by Mrs. Corbett, who thought a journey the only time to read, were thrust in like pert, undersized intruders among the respectable nineteenth-century works of culture, chastely bound in dark blue or green, which Mr. Corbett had considered the right thing to buy during his Oxford days; beside these there swaggered the children's large gaily bound story-books and collections of Fairy Tales in every colour.

From among this neat new cloth-bound crowd there towered here and there a musty sepulchre of learning, brown with the colour of dust rather than leather, with no trace of gilded letters, however faded, on its crumbling back to tell what lay inside. A few of these moribund survivors from the Dean's library were inhospitably fastened with rusty clasps; all remained closed, and appeared impenetrable, their blank, forbidding backs uplifted above their frivolous surroundings with the air of scorn that belongs to a private and concealed knowledge. For only the worm of corruption now bored his way through their evil-smelling pages.

It was an unusual flight of fancy for Mr. Corbett to imagine that the vaporous and fog-ridden air that seemed to hang more thickly about the bookcase was like a dank and poisonous breath exhaled by one or other of these slowly rotting volumes. Discomfort in this pervasive and impalpable presence came on him more acutely than at any time that day; in an attempt to clear his throat of it he choked most unpleasantly.

He hurriedly chose a Dickens from the second shelf as appropriate to a London fog, and had returned to the foot of the stairs when he decided that his reading tonight should by contrast be of blue Italian skies and white statues, in beautiful rhythmic sentences. He went back for a Walter Pater.

He found *Marius the Epicurean* tipped sideways across the gap left by his withdrawal of *The Old Curiosity Shop*. It was a very wide gap to have been left by a single volume, for the books on that shelf had been closely wedged together. He put the Dickens back into it and saw that there was still space for a large book. He said to himself in careful and precise words: "This is nonsense. No one can possibly have gone into the dining-room and removed a book while I was crossing the hall. There must have been a gap before in the second shelf." But another part of his mind kept saying in a hurried, tumbled torrent: "There was no gap in the second shelf. There was no gap in the second shelf."

He snatched at both the *Marius* and *The Old Curiosity Shop*, and went to his room in a haste that was unnecessary and absurd, since even if he believed in ghosts, which he did not, no one had the smallest reason for suspecting any in the modern Kensington house wherein he and his family had lived for the last fifteen years. Reading was the best thing to calm the nerves, and Dickens a pleasant, wholesome and robust author.

Tonight, however, Dickens struck him in a different light. Beneath the author's sentimental pity for the weak and helpless, he could discern a revolting pleasure in cruelty and suffering, while the grotesque figures of the people in Cruikshank's illustrations revealed too clearly the hideous distortions of their souls. What had seemed humorous now appeared diabolic, and in disgust at these two favourites he turned to Walter Pater for the repose and dignity of a classic spirit.

But presently he wondered if this spirit were not in itself of a marble quality, frigid and lifeless, contrary to the purpose of nature. "I have often thought," he said to himself, "that there is something evil in the austere worship of beauty for its own sake." He had never thought so before, but he liked to think that this impulse of fancy was the result of mature consideration, and with this satisfaction he composed himself for sleep.

He woke two or three times in the night, an unusual occurrence, but he was glad of it, for each time he had been dreaming horribly of these blameless Victorian works. Sprightly devils in whiskers and peg-top trousers tortured a lovely maiden and leered in delight at her anguish; the gods and heroes of classic fable acted deeds whose naked crime and shame Mr. Corbett had never appreciated in Latin and Greek Unseens. When he had woken in a cold sweat from the spectacle of the ravished Philomel's torn and bleeding tongue, he decided there was nothing for it but to go down and get another book that would turn his thoughts in some more pleasant direction. But his increasing reluctance to do this found a hundred excuses.

The recollection of the gap in the shelf now occurred to him with a sense of unnatural importance; in the troubled dozes that followed, this gap between two books seemed the most hideous deformity, like a gap between the front teeth of some grinning monster.

But in the clear daylight of the morning Mr. Corbett came down to the pleasant dining-room, its sunny windows and smell of coffee and toast, and ate an undiminished breakfast with a mind chiefly occupied in self-congratulation that the wind had blown the fog away in time for his Saturday game of golf. Whistling happily, he was pouring out his final cup of coffee when his hand remained arrested in the act as his glance, roving across the book-case, noticed that there was now no gap at all in the second shelf. He asked who had been at the bookcase already, but neither of the girls had, nor Dicky, and Mrs. Corbett was not yet down. The maid never touched the books. They wanted to know what book he missed in it, which made him look foolish, as he could not say. The things that disturb us at midnight are negligible at 9 a.m.

"I thought there was a gap in the second shelf," he said, "but it doesn't matter."

"There never is a gap in the second shelf," said little Jean brightly. "You can take out lots of books from it and when you go back the gap's always filled up. Haven't you noticed that? I have."

Nora, the middle one in age, said Jean was always being silly; she had been found crying over the funny pictures in *The Rose and the Ring* because she said all the people in them had such wicked faces, and the picture of a black cat had upset her because she thought it was a witch. Mr. Corbett did not like to think of such fancies for his Jeannie. She retaliated briskly by saying Dicky was just as bad, and he was a big boy. He had kicked a book across the room and said, "Filthy stuff," just like that. Jean was a good mimic; her tone expressed a venom of disgust, and she made the gesture of dropping a book as though the very touch of it were loathsome. Dicky, who had been making violent signs at her, now told her she was a beastly little sneak and he would never again take her for rides on the step of his bicycle. Mr. Corbett was disturbed. Unpleasant housemaids and bad schoolfriends passed through his head, as he gravely asked his son how he had got hold of this book.

"Took it out of that bookcase of course," said Dicky furiously.

It turned out to be the *Boy's Gulliver's Travels* that Granny had given him, and Dicky had at last to explain his rage with the devil who wrote it to show that men were worse than beasts and the human race a wash-out. A boy who never had good school reports had no right to be so morbidly sensitive as to penetrate to the underlying cynicism of Swift's delightful fable, and that moreover in the bright and carefully expurgated edition they bring out nowadays. Mr. Corbett could not say he had ever noticed the cynicism himself, though he knew from the critical books it must be there, and with some annoyance he advised his son to take out a nice bright modern boy's adventure story that could not depress anybody. It appeared, however, that Dicky was "off reading just now", and the girls echoed this.

Mr. Corbett soon found that he too was "off reading". Every new book seemed to him weak, tasteless and insipid; while his old and familiar books were depressing or even, in some obscure way, disgusting. Authors must all be filthy-minded; they probably wrote what they dared not express in their lives. Stevenson had said that literature was a morbid secretion; he read Stevenson again to discover his peculiar morbidity, and detected in his essays a self-pity masquerading as courage, and in *Treasure Island* an invalid's sickly attraction to brutality.

This gave him a zest to find out what he disliked so much, and his taste for reading revived as he explored with relish the hidden infirmities of minds that had been valued by fools as great and noble. He saw Jane Austen and Charlotte Bronte as two unpleasant examples of spinsterhood; the one as a prying, sub-acid busybody in everyone else's flirtations, the other as a raving, craving maenad seeking self-immolation on the altar of her frustrated passions. He compared Wordsworth's love of nature to the monstrous egoism of an ancient bell-wether, isolated from the flock.

These powers of penetration astonished him. With a mind so acute and original he should have achieved greatness, yet he was a mere solicitor and not prosperous at that. If he had but the money, he might do something with those ivory shares, but it would be a pure gamble, and he had no luck. His natural envy of his wealthier acquaintances now mingled with a contempt for their stupidity that approached loathing. The digestion of his lunch in the City was ruined by meeting sentimental yet successful dotards whom he had once regarded as pleasant fellows. The very sight of them spoiled his game of golf, so that he came to prefer reading alone in the dining-room even on sunny afternoons.

He discovered also and with a slight shock that Mrs. Corbett had always bored him. Dicky he began actively to dislike as an impudent blockhead, and the two girls were as insipidly alike as white mice; it was a relief when he abolished their tiresome habit of coming in to say good night.

In the now unbroken silence and seclusion of the dining-room, he read with feverish haste as though he were seeking for some clue to knowledge, some secret key to existence which would quicken and inflame it, transform it from its present dull torpor to a life worthy of him and his powers.

He even explored the few decaying remains of his uncle's theological library. Bored and baffled, he yet persisted, and had the occasional relief of an ugly woodcut of Adam and Eve with figures like bolsters and hair like dahlias, or a map of the Cosmos with Hell-mouth in the corner, belching forth demons. One of these books had diagrams and symbols in the margin which he took to be mathematical formulae of a kind he did not know. He presently discovered that they were drawn, not printed, and that the book was in manuscript, in a very neat, crabbed black writing that resembled black-letter printing. It was moreover in Latin, a fact that gave Mr. Corbett a shock of unreasoning disappointment. For while examining the signs in the margin, he had been filled with an extraordinary exultation as though he knew himself to be on the edge of a discovery that should alter his whole life. But he had forgotten his Latin.

With a secret and guilty air which would have looked absurd to anyone who knew his harmless purpose, he stole to the schoolroom for Dicky's Latin dictionary and grammar and hurried back to the dining-room, where he tried to discover what the book was about with an anxious industry that surprised himself. There was no name to it, nor of the author. Several blank pages had been left at the end, and the writing ended at the bottom of a page, with no flourish or superscription, as though the book had been left unfinished. From what sentences he could translate, it seemed to be a work on theology rather than mathematics. There were constant references to the Master, to his wishes and injunctions, which appeared to be of a complicated kind. Mr. Corbett began by skipping these as mere accounts of ceremonial, but a word caught his eye as one unlikely to occur in such an account. He read this passage attentively, looking up each word in the dictionary, and could hardly believe the result of his translation. "Clearly," he decided, "this book must be by some early missionary, and the passage I have just read the account of some horrible rite practised by a savage tribe of devil-worshippers." Though he called it "horrible", he reflected on it, committing each detail to memory. He then amused himself by copying the signs in the margin near it and trying to discover their significance. But a sensation of sickly cold came over him, his head swam, and he could hardly see the figures before his eyes. He suspected a sudden attack of influenza, and went to ask his wife for medicine.

They were all in the drawing-room, Mrs. Corbett helping Nora and Jean with a new game, Dicky playing the pianola, and Mike, the Irish terrier, who had lately deserted his accustomed place on the dining-room hearthrug, stretched by the fire. Mr. Corbett had an instant's impression of this peaceful and cheerful scene, before his family turned towards him and asked in scared tones what was the matter. He thought how like sheep they looked and sounded; nothing in his appearance in the mirror struck him as odd; it was their gaping faces that were unfamiliar. He then noticed the extraordinary behaviour of Mike, who had sprung from the hearthrug and was crouched in the furthest corner, uttering no sound, but with his eyes distended and foam round his bared teeth. Under Mr. Corbett's glance, he slunk towards the door, whimpering in a faint and abject manner, and then as his master called him, he snarled horribly, and the hair bristled on the scruff of his neck. Dicky let him out, and they heard him scuffling at a frantic rate down the stairs to the kitchen, and then, again and again, a long-drawn howl.

"What *can* be the matter with Mike?" asked Mrs. Corbett.

Her question broke a silence that seemed to have lasted a long time. Jean began to cry. Mr. Corbett said irritably that he did not know what was the matter with any of them.

Then Nora asked, "What is that red mark on your face?"

He looked again in the glass and could see nothing.

"It's quite clear from here," said Dicky; "I can see the lines in the finger-print."

"Yes, that's what it is," said Mrs. Corbett in her brisk staccato voice; "the print of a finger on your forehead. Have you been writing in red ink?"

Mr. Corbett precipitately left the room for his own, where he sent down a message that he was suffering from headache and would have his dinner in bed. He wanted no one fussing round him. By next morning he was amazed at his fancies of influenza, for he had never felt so well in his life.

No one commented on his looks at breakfast, so he concluded that the mark had disappeared. The old Latin book he had been translating on the previous night had been moved from the writing bureau, although Dicky's grammar and dictionary were still there. The second shelf was, as always in the day-time, closely packed; the book had, he remembered, been in the second shelf. But this time he did not ask who had put it back.

That day he had an unexpected stroke of luck in a new client of the name of Crab, who entrusted him with large sums of money: nor was he irritated by the sight of his more prosperous acquaintances, but with difficulty refrained from grinning in their faces, so confident was he that his remarkable ability must soon place him higher than any of them. At dinner he chaffed his family with what he felt to be the gaiety of a schoolboy. But on them it had a contrary effect, for they stared, either at him in stupid astonishment, or at their plates, depressed and nervous. Did they think him drunk? he wondered, and a fury came on him at their low and bestial suspicions and heavy dullness of mind. Why, he was younger than any of them!

But in spite of this new alertness he could not attend to the letters he should have written that evening and drifted to the bookcase
for a little light distraction, but found that for the first time there
was nothing he wished to read. He pulled out a book from above
his head at random, and saw that it was the old Latin book in
manuscript. As he turned over its stiff and yellow pages, he noticed
with pleasure the smell of corruption that had first repelled him in
these decaying volumes, a smell, he now thought, of ancient and
secret knowledge.

This idea of secrecy seemed to affect him personally, for on
hearing a step in the hall he hastily closed the book and put it back
in its place. He went to the schoolroom where Dicky was doing
his home-work, and told him he required his Latin grammar and
dictionary again for an old law report. To his annoyance he stammered and put his words awkwardly; he thought that the boy
looked oddly at him and he cursed him in his heart for a suspicious
young devil, though of what he should be suspicious he could not
say. Nevertheless, when back in the dining-room, he listened at the
door and then softly turned the lock before he opened the books
on the writing-bureau.

The script and Latin seemed much clearer than on the previous
evening, and he was able to read at random a passage relating to a
trial of a German midwife in 1620 for the murder and dissection of
783 children. Even allowing for the opportunities afforded by her
profession, the number appeared excessive, nor could he discover
any motive for the slaughter. He decided to translate the book
from the beginning.

It appeared to be an account of some secret society whose
activities and ritual were of a nature so obscure, and when not, so
vile and terrible, that Mr. Corbett would not at first believe that this

could be a record of any human mind, although his deep interest
in it should have convinced him that from his humanity at least it
was not altogether alien.

He read until far later than his usual hour for bed and when at
last he rose, it was with the book in his hands. To defer his parting
with it, he stood turning over the pages until he reached the end
of the writing, and was struck by a new peculiarity.

The ink was much fresher and of a far poorer quality than the
thick rusted ink in the bulk of the book; on close inspection he
would have said that it was of modern manufacture and written
quite recently were it not for the fact that it was in the same crabbed
late seventeenth-century handwriting.

This however did not explain the perplexity, even dismay and
fear, he now felt as he stared at the last sentence. It ran: "Confine
te in perennibus studiis," and he had at once recognised it as a
Ciceronian tag that had been dinned into him at school. He could
not understand how he had failed to notice it yesterday.

Then he remembered that the book had ended at the bottom
of a page. But now, the last two sentences were written at the very
top of a page. However long he looked at them, he could come
to no other conclusion than that they had been added since the
previous evening.

He now read the sentence before the last: "Re imperfecta mor-
tuus sum," and translated the whole as: "I died with my purpose
unachieved. Continue, thou, the never-ending studies."

With his eyes still fixed upon it, Mr. Corbett replaced the book
on the writing-bureau and stepped back from it to the door, his
hand outstretched behind him, groping and then tugging at the
door-handle. As the door failed to open, his breath came in a faint,
hardly articulate scream. Then he remembered that he had himself

locked it, and he fumbled with the key in frantic ineffectual movements until at last he opened it and banged it after him as he plunged
backwards into the hall.

For a moment he stood there looking at the door-handle; then
with a stealthy, sneaking movement, his hand crept out towards it,
touched it, began to turn it, when suddenly he pulled his hand away
and went up to his bedroom, three steps at a time.

There he behaved in a manner only comparable with the way
he had lost his head after losing his innocence when a schoolboy of
sixteen. He hid his face in the pillow, he cried, he raved in meaningless words, repeating: "Never, never, never. I will never do it again.
Help me never to do it again." With the words, "Help me," he
noticed what he was saying, they reminded him of other words,
and he began to pray aloud. But the words sounded jumbled, they
persisted in coming into his head in a reverse order so that he found
he was saying his prayers backwards, and at this final absurdity he
suddenly began to laugh very loud. He sat up on the bed, delighted
at this return to sanity, common sense and humour, when the door
leading into Mrs. Corbett's room opened, and he saw his wife staring at him with a strange, grey, drawn face that made her seem
like the terror-stricken ghost of her usually smug and placid self.

"It's not burglars," he said irritably. "I've come to bed late, that
is all, and must have waked you."

"Henry," said Mrs. Corbett, and he noticed that she had not
heard him, "Henry, didn't you hear it?"

"What?"

"That laugh."

He was silent, an instinctive caution warning him to wait until
she spoke again. And this she did, imploring him with her eyes to
reassure her.

"It was not a human laugh. It was like the laugh of a devil."

He checked his violent inclination to laugh again. It was wiser not to let her know that it was only his laughter she had heard. He told her to stop being fanciful, and Mrs. Corbett, gradually recovering her docility, returned to obey an impossible command, since she could not stop being what she had never been.

The next morning, Mr. Corbett rose before any of the servants and crept down to the dining-room. As before, the dictionary and grammar alone remained on the writing-bureau; the book was back in the second shelf. He opened it at the end. Two more lines had been added, carrying the writing down to the middle of the page. They ran:

> *Ex auro canceris*
> *In dentem elephantis.*

which he translated as:

> *Out of the money of the crab*
> *Into the tooth of the elephant.*

From this time on, his acquaintances in the City noticed a change in the mediocre, rather flabby and unenterprising "old Corbett". His recent sour depression dropped from him: he seemed to have grown twenty years younger, strong, brisk and cheerful, and with a self-confidence in business that struck them as lunacy. They waited with a not unpleasant excitement for the inevitable crash, but his every speculation, however wild and hare-brained, turned out successful. He no longer avoided them, but went out of his way to display his consciousness of luck, daring and vigour, and to chaff them in a manner that began to make him actively disliked. This he welcomed with delight as a sign of others' envy and his superiority.

He never stayed in town for dinners or theatres, for he was always now in a hurry to get home, where, as soon as he was sure of being undisturbed, he would take down the manuscript book from the second shelf of the dining-room and turn to the last pages.

Every morning he found that a few words had been added since the evening before, and always they formed, as he considered, injunctions to himself. These were at first only with regard to his money transactions, giving assurance to his boldest fancies, and since the brilliant and unforeseen success that had attended his gamble with Mr. Crab's money in African ivory, he followed all such advice unhesitatingly.

But presently, interspersed with these commands, were others of a meaningless, childish, yet revolting character such as might be invented by a decadent imbecile, or, it must be admitted, by the idle fancies of any ordinary man who permits his imagination to wander unbridled. Mr. Corbett was startled to recognise one or two such fancies of his own, which had occurred to him during his frequent boredom in church, and which he had not thought any other mind could conceive.

He at first paid no attention to these directions, but found that his new speculations declined so rapidly that he became terrified not merely for his fortune but for his reputation and even safety, since the money of various of his clients was involved. It was made clear to him that he must follow the commands in the book altogether or not at all, and he began to carry out their puerile and grotesque blasphemies with a contemptuous amusement, which however gradually changed to a sense of their monstrous significance. They became more capricious and difficult of execution, but he now never hesitated to obey blindly, urged by a fear that he could not understand, but knew only that it was not of mere financial failure.

By now he understood the effect of this book on the others near it, and the reason that had impelled its mysterious agent to move the books into the second shelf so that all in turn should come under the influence of that ancient and secret knowledge.

In respect to it, he encouraged his children, with jeers at their stupidity, to read more, but he could not observe that they ever now took a book from the dining-room bookcase. He himself no longer needed to read, but went to bed early and slept sound. The things that all his life he had longed to do when he should have enough money now seemed to him insipid. His most exciting pleasure was the smell and touch of these mouldering pages as he turned them to find the last message inscribed to him.

One evening it was in two words only: "Canem occide."

He laughed at this simple and pleasant request to kill the dog, for he bore Mike a grudge for his change from devotion to slinking aversion. Moreover, it could not have come more opportunely, since in turning out an old desk he had just discovered some packets of rat poison bought years ago and forgotten. No one therefore knew of its existence and it would be easy to poison Mike without any further suspicion than that of a neighbour's carelessness. He whistled light-heartedly as he ran upstairs to rummage for the packets, and returned to empty one in the dog's dish of water in the hall.

That night the household was awakened by terrified screams proceeding from the stairs. Mr. Corbett was the first to hasten there, prompted by the instinctive caution that was always with him these days. He saw Jean, in her nightdress, scrambling up on to the landing on her hands and knees, clutching at anything that afforded support and screaming in a choking, tearless, unnatural manner. He carried her to the room she shared with Nora, where they were quickly followed by Mrs. Corbett.

Nothing coherent could be got from Jean. Nora said that she must have been having her old dream again; when her father demanded what this was, she said that Jean sometimes woke in the night, crying, because she had dreamed of a hand passing backwards and forwards over the dining-room bookcase, until it found a certain book and took it out of the shelf. At this point she was always so frightened that she woke up.

On hearing this, Jean broke into fresh screams, and Mrs. Corbett would have no more explanations. Mr. Corbett went out on to the stairs to find what had brought the child there from her bed. On looking down into the lighted hall, he saw Mike's dish overturned. He went down to examine it and saw that the water he had poisoned must have been upset and absorbed by the rough doormat which was quite wet.

He went back to the little girls' room, told his wife that she was tired and must go to bed, and he would take his turn at comforting Jean. She was now much quieter. He took her on his knee where at first she shrank from him. Mr. Corbett remembered with an angry sense of injury that she never now sat on his knee, and would have liked to pay her out for it by mocking and frightening her. But he had to coax her into telling him what he wanted, and with this object he soothed her, calling her by pet names that he thought he had forgotten, telling her that nothing could hurt her now he was with her.

At first his cleverness amused him; he chuckled softly when Jean buried her head in his dressing-gown. But presently an uncomfortable sensation came over him, he gripped at Jean as though for her protection, while he was so smoothly assuring her of his. With difficulty, he listened to what he had at last induced her to tell him.

She and Nora had kept Mike with them all the evening and taken him to sleep in their room for a treat. He had lain at the foot of Jean's bed and they had all gone to sleep. Then Jean began her old dream of the hand moving over the books in the dining-room bookcase; but instead of taking out a book, it came across the dining-room and out on to the stairs. It came up over the banisters and to the door of their room, and turned their door-handle very softly and opened it. At this point she jumped up wide awake and turned on the light, calling to Nora. The door, which had been shut when they went to sleep, was wide open, and Mike was gone.

She told Nora that she was sure something dreadful would happen to him if she did not go and bring him back, and ran down into the hall where she saw him just about to drink from his dish. She called to him and he looked up, but did not come, so she ran to him, and began to pull him along with her, when her nightdress was clutched from behind and then she felt a hand seize her arm.

She fell down, and then clambered upstairs as fast as she could, screaming all the way.

It was now clear to Mr. Corbett that Mike's dish must have been upset in the scuffle. She was again crying, but this time he felt himself unable to comfort her. He retired to his room, where he walked up and down in an agitation he could not understand, for he found his thoughts perpetually arguing on a point that had never troubled him before.

"I am not a bad man," he kept saying to himself. "I have never done anything actually wrong. My clients are none the worse for my speculations, only the better. Nor have I spent my new wealth on gross and sensual pleasures; these now have even no attraction for me."

Presently he added: "It is not wrong to try and kill a dog, an ill-tempered brute. It turned against me. It might have bitten Jeannie."

He noticed that he had thought of her as Jeannie, which he had not done for some time; it must have been because he had called her that tonight. He must forbid her ever to leave her room at night, he could not have her meddling. It would be safer for him if she were not there at all.

Again that sick and cold sensation of fear swept over him: he seized the bed-post as though he were falling, and held on to it for some minutes. "I was thinking of a boarding school," he told himself, and then, "I must go down and find out—find out—" He would not think what it was he must find out.

He opened his door and listened. The house was quiet. He crept on to the landing and along to Nora's and Jean's door where again he stood, listening. There was no sound, and at that he was again overcome with unreasonable terror. He imagined Jean lying very still in her bed, too still. He hastened away from the door, shuffling in his bedroom slippers along the passage and down the stairs.

A bright fire still burned in the dining-room grate. A glance at the clock told him it was not yet twelve. He stared at the bookcase. In the second shelf was a gap which had not been there when he had left. On the writing-bureau lay a large open book. He knew that he must cross the room and see what was written in it. Then, as before, words that he did not intend came sobbing and crying to his lips, muttering, "No, no, not that. Never, never, never." But he crossed the room and looked down at the book. As last time, the message was in only two words: "Infantem occide."

He slipped and fell forward against the bureau. His hands clutched at the book, lifted it as he recovered himself and with his finger he traced out the words that had been written. The smell of corruption crept into his nostrils. He told himself that he was not a snivelling dotard, but a man stronger and wiser than his fellows, superior to the common emotions of humanity, who held in his hands the sources of ancient and secret power.

He had known what the message would be. It was after all the only safe and logical thing to do. Jean had acquired dangerous knowledge. She was a spy, an antagonist. That she was so unconsciously, that she was eight years old, his youngest and favourite child, were sentimental appeals that could make no difference to a man of sane reasoning power such as his own. Jean had sided with Mike against him. "All that are not with me are against me," he repeated softly. He would kill both dog and child with the white powder that no one knew to be in his possession. It would be quite safe.

He laid down the book and went to the door. What he had to do, he would do quickly, for again that sensation of deadly cold was sweeping over him. He wished he had not to do it tonight; last night it would have been easier, but tonight she had sat on his knee and made him afraid. He imagined her lying very still in her bed, too still. But it would be she who would lie there, not he, so why should he be afraid? He was protected by ancient and secret powers. He held on to the door-handle, but his fingers seemed to have grown numb, for he could not turn it. He clung to it, crouched and shivering, bending over it until he knelt on the ground, his head beneath the handle which he still clutched with upraised hands. Suddenly the hands were loosened and flung outwards with the frantic gesture of a man falling from a great height, and he stumbled to his feet.

He seized the book and threw it on the fire. A violent sensation of choking overcame him, he felt he was being strangled, as in a nightmare he tried again and again to shriek aloud, but his breath would make no sound. His breath would not come at all. He fell backwards heavily, down on the floor, where he lay very still.

In the morning, the maid who came to open the dining-room windows found her master dead. The sensation caused by this was scarcely so great in the City as that given by the simultaneous collapse of all Mr. Corbett's recent speculations. It was instantly assumed that he must have had previous knowledge of this and so committed suicide.

The stumbling-block to this theory was that the medical report defined the cause of Mr. Corbett's death as strangulation of the wind-pipe by the pressure of a hand which had left the marks of its fingers on his throat.

THE APPLE TREE (1931)

Elizabeth Bowen (1899–1973)

Elizabeth Dorothea Cole Bowen was born in Dublin but lived for most of her life in England. Her most famous novels include *The Death of the Heart* (1938) and *The Heat of the Day* (1949), both of which explore the theme of loneliness—the former between the wars, and the latter against the backdrop of the London Blitz. She did not use supernatural tropes in her novels, but was an enthusiastic writer of short ghost stories, seeing them as a perfect way of manifesting the problems and uncertainties of the modern world. She explains in her introduction to Cynthia Asquith's anthology *The Second Ghost Book* (1952):

> Ghosts have grown up. Far behind lie their clanking and moaning days; they have laid aside their original bag of tricks—bleeding hands, luminous skulls and so on. Their manifestations are, like their personalities, oblique and subtle, perfectly calculated to get the modern person under the skin. They abjure the over-fantastic and grotesque, operating, instead, through series of happenings whose horror lies in their being just, *just* out of the true... Ghosts draw us together: one might leave it at that. Can there be something tonic about pure, active fear in these times of passive, confused oppression? It is nice to *choose* to be frightened, when one need not be. Or it may be that, deadened by information,

we are glad of these awful, intent and nameless beings as to whom no information is to be had. Our irrational, darker selves demand familiars.

In 1912, when Bowen was thirteen years old, her mother died of cancer. The inevitable impression this left on her caused her to populate her stories with many orphaned children. 'The Apple Tree' deals with a traumatic incident which happens to a girl when she is twelve, and how it affects the rest of her life. It was first published in another Cynthia Asquith collection, *When Churchyards Yawn*, in 1931.

"FRIGHTENED?" EXCLAIMED LANCELOT, "OF HER? OH, NON-sense—surely? She's an absolute child."

"But *that's* what I mean," said Mrs. Bettersley, glancing queerly sideways at him over the collar of her fur coat. He still did not know what she meant, and did not think she knew either.

In a rather nerve-racking combination of wind and moon-light Simon Wing's week-end party picked its way back to his house, by twos and threes, up a cinder-path from the village. Simon, who entered with gusto into his new rôle of squire, had insisted that they should attend the Saturday concert in the village memorial hall, a raftered, charmless and icy building endowed by himself, and only recently opened. Here, with numbing feet and creeping spines, they had occupied seven front seats, under a thin but constant spate of recitation, pianoforte duet and song, while upon them from all quarters draughts directed themselves like arrows. To restore circulation they had applauded vigor-ously, too often precipitating an encore. Simon, satisfied with his friends, with his evening, leant forward to beam down the row. He said this would please the village. Lancelot communi-cated to Mrs. Bettersley a suspicion; this was why Simon had asked them down.

"So I'm afraid," she replied, "and for church tomorrow."

All the same it had warmed them all to see Simon happy. Mounting the platform to propose a vote of thanks to the vicar, the great ruddy man had positively expanded; glowed; a till now too palpable cloud rolled away from him. It was this recognition by his old friends of the old Simon—a recognition so instantaneous, poignant and cheerful that it was like a handshake, a first greeting— that now sent the party so cheerfully home in its twos and threes, their host ever boisterously ahead. At the tail, lagging, Lancelot and Mrs. Bettersley fell into a discussion of Simon (his marriage, his ménage, his whole aspect) marked by entire unrestraint; as though between these two also some shadow had dissipated. They were old, friendly enemies.

"But a child—" resumed Lancelot.

"Naturally I didn't mean to suggest that she was a werewolf!"

"You think she *is* what's the matter?"

"Obviously there's nothing funny about the house."

Obviously there was nothing funny about the house. Under the eery cold sky, pale but not bright with moonlight, among bare wind-shaken trees, the house's bulk loomed, honourably substantial. Lit-up windows sustained the party with promise of indoor comfort: firelight on decanters, room after room heavy-curtained; Simon's feeling for home made concrete (at last, after wandering years) in deep leather chairs, padded fenders and sectional bookcases, "domes of silence" on yielding carpets; an unaspiring, comfortable sobriety.

"She does seem to me only half there," confessed Lancelot; "not, of course, I mean mentally, but—"

"She had that frightful time—don't you know? *Don't* you know?" Mrs. Bettersley brightened, approaching her lips to his ear in the half moonlight. "She was at that school—don't you remember? After all *that,* the school broke up, you know. She was sent straight abroad—she'd have been twelve at the time, I dare say—in a pretty state, I've no doubt, poor child!—to an aunt and uncle at Cannes. Her only relations; they lived out there in a villa, never came home—she stayed abroad with them. It was then Simon met her; then—all this."

"School?" said Lancelot, stuttering with excitement. "What—were they ill-treated?"

"Heavens, not that," exclaimed Mrs. Bettersley; "worse—"

But just at this point—it was unbearable—they saw the party pull up and contract ahead. Simon was waiting to shepherd them through the gate, to lock the gate after them.

"I hope," he said, beaming, as they came up, "you weren't too bored?"

They could not fail to respond.

"It's been a marvellous evening," said Mrs. Bettersley; Lancelot adding, "What wonderful talent you've got round here."

"I don't think we're bad for a village," said Simon modestly, clicking the gate to. "The choral society are as keen as mustard. And I always think that young Dickinson ought to go on the stage. I'd pay to see him anywhere."

"Oh, so would I," agreed Lancelot cordially. "It's too sad," he added, "your wife having missed all this."

Simon's manner contracted. "She went to the dress rehearsal," he said quickly.

"Doesn't she act herself?"

"I can't get her to try... Well, here we are; here we are!" Simon shouted, stamping across the terrace.

Young Mrs. Wing had been excused the concert. She had a slight chill, she feared. If she ever did cast any light on village society it was to-night withheld. No doubt Simon was disappointed. His friends, filing after him through the french window into the library, all hoped that by now—it was half-past ten—young Mrs. Simon might have taken her chill to bed.

But from the hearth her flat little voice said "Hullo!" There she still stood, looking towards the window, watching their entrance as she had watched their exit. Her long silver sheath of a dress made her almost grown up. So they all prepared with philosophy to be nice to young Mrs. Wing. They all felt this first week-end party, this incursion of old friends all knit up with each other, so knit up round Simon, might well be trying for young Mrs. Wing. In the nature, even possibly, of an ordeal. She was barely nineteen, and could not, to meet them, be expected to put up anything of "a manner". She had them, however, at a slight disadvantage, for Simon's marriage had been a shock for his friends. He had been known for years as a likely marrying man; so much so that his celibacy appeared an accident; but his choice of a wife—this mannerless, sexless child, the dim something between a mouse and an Undine, this wraith not considerable as a mother of sons, this cold little shadow across a hearth—had considerably surprised them. By her very passivity she attacked them when they were least prepared.

Mrs. Wing, at a glance from her husband, raised a silver lid from some sandwiches with a gesture of invitation. Mrs. Bettersley, whose appetite was frankly wolfish, took two, and slipping out inch by inch from her fur coat, lined up beside her little hostess in the firelight, solid and brilliant. The others divided armchairs in the circle of warmth.

"Did you have a nice concert?" said Mrs. Wing politely. No one could answer. "It went off well on the whole," said Simon gently, as though breaking sorrowful news to her.

Lancelot could not sleep. The very comfort of bed, the too exquisite sympathy with his body of springs and mattress, became oppressive. Wind had subsided, moonlight sketched a window upon his floor. The house was quiet, too quiet; with jealousy and nostalgia he pictured them all sleeping. Mrs. Wing's cheek would scarcely warm a pillow. In despair Lancelot switched the light on; the amiable furniture stared. He read one page of *Our Mutual Friend* with distaste and decided to look downstairs for a detective story. He slept in a corridor branching off from the head of the main staircase.

Downstairs the hall was dark, rank with cooling cigar-smoke. A clock struck three; Lancelot violently started. A little moon came in through the skylight; the library door was closed; stepping quietly Lancelot made his way to it. He opened the door, saw red embers, then knew in a second the library was not empty. All the same, in there in the dark they were not moving or speaking.

Embarrassment—had he surprised an intrigue?—and abrupt physical fear—were these burglars?—held Lancelot bound on the threshold. Certainly someone was not alone; in here, in spite of the dark, someone was watching someone. He did not know whether to speak. He felt committed by opening the door, and standing against the grey of the glass-roofed fall must be certainly visible.

Finally it was Simon's voice that said defensively: "Hullo?" Lancelot knew he must go away immediately. He had only one wish—to conceal his identity. But Simon apparently did not trust one; moving bulkily he came down the long room to the door, bumping, as though in a quite unfamiliar room, against the furniture, his arm out ahead, as though pushing aside or trying to part a curtain. He seemed to have no sense of distance; Lancelot ducked, but a great hand touched his face. The hand was ice-cold.

"Oh, you?" said Simon. From his voice, his breath, he had been drinking heavily. He must still be holding a glass in his other hand—Lancelot heard whisky slopping about as the glass shook.

"It's all right," said Lancelot; "I was just going up. Sorry," he added.

"You can't—come—in—here," said Simon obstinately.

"No, I say; I was just going up." Lancelot stopped; friendliness fought in him with an intense repulsion. Not that he minded—though this itself was odd; Simon hardly ever touched anything.

But the room was a trap, a cul-de-sac; Simon, his face less than a yard away, seemed to be speaking to him through bars. He was frightful in fear; a man with the humility of a beast; he gave off fear like some disagreeable animal smell, making Lancelot dislike and feel revolted by his own humanity, his own manhood.

"Go away," said Simon, pushing at him in the dark. Lancelot stepped back in alarm, a rug slipped under his foot, he staggered, grasping at the lintel of the door. His elbow knocked a switch; immediately the hall, with its four hanging lamps, sprang into brilliant illumination. One was staggered by this explosion of light; Lancelot put his hands over his eyes; when he took them away he could see Simon's face was clammy, mottled; here and there a bead of sweat trembled and ran down. He was standing sideways, his shoulder against the door; past him a path of light ran into the library.

Mrs. Simon stood just out of the light, looking fixedly up and pointing at something above her head. Round her Lancelot distinguished the big chairs, the table with the decanters, and, faintly, the glazed bookcases. Her eyes, looking up, reflected the light but did not flicker; she did not stir. With an exclamation, a violent movement, Simon shut the library door. They both stood outside its white glossy panels. By contrast with what stood inside, staring there in the dark, Simon was once more human; unconsciously, as much to gain as to impart reassurance, Lancelot put a hand on his arm.

Not looking at one another, they said nothing.

They were in no sense alone even here, for the slam of the door produced in a moment or two Mrs. Bettersley, who looked down at them from the gallery just overhead the zone of bright lights, her face sharpened and wolfish from vehement curiosity. Lancelot looked up; their eyes met.

"All right, only somebody sleep-walking," he called up softly.

"All right," she replied, withdrawing; but not, he guessed, to her room; rather to lean back in shadow against the wall of the gallery, impassive, watchful, arms folded over the breast of her dark silk kimono.

A moment later she still made no sign—he would have been glad of her presence. For the return to Simon of sensibility and intelligence, like circulation beginning again in a limb that had been tightly bound up, was too much for Simon. One side glance that almost contained his horror, then—huge figure, crumpling, swaying, sagging—he fainted suddenly. Lancelot broke his fall a little and propped him, sitting, against the wall.

This left Lancelot much alone. He noted details: a dog-collar lying unstrapped, ash trodden into a rug, a girl's gloves—probably Mrs. Simon's—dropped crumpled into a big brass tray. Now drawn to the door—aware the whole time of his position's absurdity—he knelt, one ear to the keyhole. Silence. In there she must still stand in contemplation—horrified, horrifying—of something high up that from the not-quite fixity of her gaze had seemed unfixed, pendant, perhaps swaying a little. Silence. Then—he pressed closer—a thud—thud—thud—three times, like apples falling.

This idea of apples entered his mind and remained, frightfully clear; an innocent pastoral image seen black through a dark transparency. This idea of fruit detaching itself and, from a leafy height, falling in the stale, shut-up room, had the sharpness of an hallucination; he thought he was going mad.

"Come down," he called up to the gallery.

Mrs. Bettersley, with that expectant half-smile, appeared immediately and came downstairs. She glanced at Simon's unconsciousness, for which she seemed to be grateful, then went to the library door. After a moment facing the panels she tried the handle, cautiously turning it.

"*She's* in there," said Lancelot.

"Coming?" she asked.

He replied "No," very frankly and simply.

"Oh, well," she shrugged; "I'm a woman," and entered the library, pushing the door to behind her. He heard her moving among the furniture. "Now come," she said. "Come, my dear..." After a moment or two of complete silence and stillness: "Oh, my God, no—I can't!" she exclaimed. She came out again, very white. She was rubbing her hands together as though she had hurt them. "It's impossible," she repeated. "One can't get past... it's like an apple tree."

She knelt by Simon and began fumbling with his collar. Her hands shook. Lancelot watched the access of womanly busyness.

The door opened again and young Mrs. Wing came out in her nightgown, hair hanging over her shoulders in two plaits, blinking under the strong light. Seeing them all, she paused in natural confusion.

"I walk in my sleep," she murmured, blushed and slipped past upstairs without a glance at her husband, still in confusion like any young woman encountered by strangers in her nightgown;

her appearance and disappearance the very picture of modest precipitancy.

Simon began to come to. Mrs. Bettersley also retreated. The fewest possible people ought, they felt, to be in on this.

Sunday morning was pale-blue, mild and sunny. Mrs. Bettersley appeared punctually for breakfast, beaming, pink and impassible. Lancelot looked pale and puffy; Mrs. Simon did not appear. Simon came in like a tempered Boreas to greet the party, rubbing his hands. After breakfast they stepped out through the window to smoke on the terrace. Church, said Simon pressingly, would be at eleven.

Mrs. Bettersley revolted. She said she liked to write letters on Sunday morning. The rest, with a glance of regret at the shining November garden, went off like lambs. When they had gone she slipped upstairs and tapped on Mrs. Simon's door.

The young woman was lying comfortably enough, with a fire burning; a mild novel open face down on the counterpane. This pretty bride's room, pink and white, frilled and rosy, now full of church bells and winter sunshine, had for Mrs. Bettersley, in all its appointments, an air of anxious imitation and approximation to some idea of the grown-up. Simon's bed was made and the room in order.

"You don't mind?" said Mrs. Bettersley, having sat down firmly.

Mrs. Simon said nervously, she was so pleased.

"All right this morning?"

"Just a little chill, I think."

"And no wonder! Do you often walk in your sleep?"

Mrs. Simon's small face tightened, hardened, went a shade whiter among the pillows. "I don't know," she said. Her manner became a positive invitation to Mrs. Bettersley to go away. Flattening among the bedclothes she tried hard to obliterate herself.

Her visitor, who had not much time—for the bells stopped, they would be back again in an hour—was quite merciless. "How old were you?" she said, "when *that* happened?"

"Twelve—please don't—"

"You never told anyone?"

"No—please, Mrs. Bettersley—please, not now, I feel so ill."

"You're making Simon ill."

"Do you think I don't know!" the child exclaimed. "I thought he'd save me. I didn't think he'd ever be frightened. I didn't know any power could... Indeed, indeed, Mrs. Bettersley, I had no idea... I felt so safe with him. I thought this would go away. Now when it comes it is twice as horrible. Do you think it is killing him?"

"I shouldn't wonder," said Mrs. Bettersley.

"Oh, oh," moaned Mrs. Wing, and with wrists crossed over her face shook all over, sobbing so that the bedhead rattled against the wall. "He was so sorry for me," she moaned; "it was more than I could resist. He was so sorry for me. Wouldn't you feel Simon might save you?"

Mrs. Bettersley, moving to the edge of the bed, caught the girl's wrists and firmly, but not untenderly, forced them apart, disclosing the small convulsed face and fixed eyes. "We've got three-quarters of an hour alone," she said. "You've got to tell me. Make it come into words. Once it's out it won't hurt—like a tooth, you know. Talk about it like anything. Talk to Simon. You never have, have you? You never do?"

Mrs. Bettersley felt quite a brute, she told Lancelot later. She had, naturally, in taking this hard line, something to go on. Seven years ago, newspapers had been full of the Crampton Park School tragedy; a little girl's suicide. There had been some remarkable headlines, some details, profuse speculation. Influence from some direction having been brought to bear, the affair disappeared from the papers abruptly. Some suggestion of things having been "hushed up" gave the affair, in talk, a fresh cruel prominence; it became a topic. One hinted at all sorts of scandal. The school broke up, the staff disappeared, discredited; the fine house and grounds, in the West Country, were sold at a loss. One pupil, Myra Conway, felt the shock with surprising keenness. She nearly died of brain fever; collapsing the day after the suicide, she remained at death's door for weeks, alone with her nurses in the horrified house, Crampton Park. All the other children were hurried away. One heard afterwards that her health, her nerves had been ruined. The other children presumably rallied; one heard no more of them. Myra Conway became Myra Wing. So much they all knew, even Simon.

Myra Wing now lay on her side in bed, in her pink bedroom, eyes shut, cheek pressed to the pillow as though she were sleeping, but with her body rigid; gripping with both hands Mrs. Bettersley's arm. She spoke slowly, choosing her words with diffidence as though hampered by trying to speak an unfamiliar language.

"I went there when I was ten. I don't think it can ever have been a very good school. They called it a home school, I suppose, because most of us stayed for the holidays—we had no parents—and none of us were over fourteen. From being there so much, we began to feel that this was the world. There was a very high wall round the garden. I don't think they were unkind to us, but everything seemed to go wrong. Doria and I were always in trouble. I suppose that was why we knew each other. There were about eighteen other girls, but none of them liked us. We used to feel we had some disease—so much so, that we were sometimes ashamed to meet each other; sometimes we did not like to be together. I don't think we knew we were unhappy; we never spoke of that; we should have felt ashamed. We used to pretend we were all right; we got in a way to be quite proud of ourselves, of being different. I think, though, we made each other worse. In those days I was very ugly. Doria was as bad; she was very queer-looking; her eyes goggled and she wore big round glasses. I suppose if we had had parents it would have been different. As it was, it was impossible to believe anyone could ever care for either of us. We did not even care for each other; we were just like two patients in hospital, shut away from the others because of having some frightful disease. But I suppose we depended on one another.

"The other children were mostly younger. The house was very large and dark-looking, but full of pictures to make it look homely. The grounds were very large, full of trees and laurels. When I was twelve, I felt if this was the world I could not bear it. When I was twelve I got measles; another girl of my age got the measles too, and we were sent to a cottage to get well. She was very pretty and clever; we made friends; she told me she did not mind me, but she could not bear Doria. When we both got well and went back to the others, I loved her so much I felt I could not bear to part from her. She had a home of her own; she was very happy and gay; to know her and hear about her life was like heaven. I took great trouble to please her; we went on being friends. The others began to like me; I ran away from Doria. Doria was left alone. She seemed to be all that was horrible in my life; from the moment we parted things began to go right with me. I laughed at her with the others.

"The only happy part of Doria's life and mine in the bad days were the games we played and the stories we told in a lonely part of the garden, a slope of lawn with one beautiful old apple tree. Sometimes we used to climb up in the branches. Nobody else ever came there, it was like something of our own; to be there made us feel happy and dignified.

"Doria was miserable when I left her. She never wept; she used to walk about by herself. It was as though everything I had got free of had fallen on her, too; she was left with my wretchedness. When I was with the others I used to see her, always alone, watching me. One afternoon she made me come with her to the apple tree; I was sorry for her and went; when we got there I could not bear it. I was so frightened of being lost again; I said terrible things to her. I wished she was dead. You see there seemed to be no other world outside the school.

"She and I still slept in the same room, with two others. That night—there was some moon—I saw her get up. She tied the cord of her dressing-gown—it was very thick—round her waist tightly; she looked once at me, but I pretended to be asleep. She went out and did not come back. I lay—there was only a little moon—with a terrible feeling, like something tight round my throat. At last I went down to look for her. A glass door to the garden was open. I went out to look for her. She had hanged herself, you know, in the apple tree. When I first got there I saw nothing. I looked round and called her, and shook the branches, but only—it was September— two or three apples fell down. The leaves kept brushing against my face. Then I saw her. Her feet were just over my head. I parted the branches to look—there was just enough moon—the leaves brushed my face. I crept back into bed and waited. No one knew; no steps came. Next morning, of course, they did not tell us anything. They said she was ill. I pretended to know no better. I could not think of anything but the apple tree.

"While I was ill—I was very ill—I thought the leaves would choke me. Whenever I moved in bed an apple fell down. All the girls were taken away. When I got well, I found the house was empty. The first day I could, I crept out alone to look for the real apple tree. 'It is only a tree,' I thought; 'if I could see it, I should be quite well.' But the tree had been cut down. The place where it grew was filled with new turf. The nurse swore to me there had never been an apple tree there at all. She did not know—no one ever knew—I had been out that night and seen Doria.

"I expect you can guess the rest—you were there last night. You see, I am haunted. It does not matter where I am, or who I am with. Though I am married now, it is just the same. Every now and then—I don't know yet when or what brings it about—I wake to see Doria get up and tie the cord round her waist and go out. I have to go after her; there is always the apple tree. Its roots are in me. It takes all my strength, and now it's beginning to take Simon's.

"Those nights, no one can bear to be with me. Everyone who has been with me knows, but no one will speak of it. Only Simon tries to be there, those times—you saw, last night. It is impossible to be with me; I make rooms impossible. I am not like a house that can be burnt, you see, or pulled down. You know how it is—I heard you in there last night, trying to come to me—"

"I won't fail again: I've never been more ashamed," said Mrs. Bettersley.

"If I stay up here the tree grows in the room; I feel it will choke Simon. If I go out, I find it darker than all the others against the sky… This morning I have been trying to make up my mind; I must go; I must leave Simon. I see quite well this is destroying him. Seeing him with you all makes me see how he used to be, how he might

have been. You see it's hard to go. He's my life. Between all this…
we're so happy. But make me do this, Mrs. Bettersley!"

"I'll make you do one thing. Come away with me—perhaps
for only a month. My dear, if I can't do this, after last night, *I'm*
ruined," exclaimed Mrs. Bettersley.

The passion of vanity has its own depths in the spirit, and is
powerfully militant. Mrs. Bettersley, determined to vindicate herself, disappeared for some weeks with the haunted girl. Lancelot,
meanwhile, kept Simon company. From the ordeal their friend
emerged about Christmas, possibly a little harder and brighter.
If she had fought, there was not a hair displaced. She did not
mention, even to Lancelot, by what arts, night and day, by what
cynical vigilance she had succeeded in exorcizing the apple tree.
The victory aged her, but left her as disengaged as usual. Mrs.
Wing was returned to her husband. As one would expect, less and
less was seen of the couple. They disappeared into happiness: a
sublime nonentity.

HERODES REDIVIVUS (1949)

A.N.L. Munby (1913–1974)

Alan Noel Latimer Munby was a later follower of M.R. James in the antiquarian tradition. His interest in rare books was first aroused by visits to booksellers in Bristol, near Clifton College where he was at school. Between 1935 and 1947 (except for during the Second World War), he worked in the book trade, at the antiquarian book dealers Bernard Quaritch, and in the book department at Sotheby's. After the war, he became Librarian of King's College, Cambridge, the college which had formerly been home to both M.R. James and E.G. Swain. He became an important figure in the librarianship community, and was made a member of the first ever British Library Board in 1973.

Munby started writing ghost stories whilst a prisoner at Oflag VII B, a German prisoner-of-war camp near Eichstätt, after his capture at Calais in 1940. The Roman Catholic Bishop of Eichstätt, Michael Rackl, gave the prisoners access to his own printing press, and they produced a camp magazine called *Touchstone*, which contained three of Munby's tales as well as poems, illustrations and essays by other prisoners. The stories recycled Munby's own antiquarian interests and knowledge into escapist fantasy for his fellow soldiers. Later he had these tales, and others written in the same period, published as *The Alabaster Hand* (1949).

Just as in M.R. James's tales, the supernatural forces in Munby's work are not all ghosts as such. This story features a Bristol schoolboy meeting a bookseller who is rather more than he seems.

I DON'T SUPPOSE THAT MANY PEOPLE HAVE HEARD OF CHARLES Auckland, the pathologist, as he isn't the type of man who catches the public eye. What slight reputation he has got is of rather a sinister nature; for he has always tended to avoid the broad, beaten tracks of scientific research, and has branched off to bring light into certain dark cul-de-sacs of the human mind, which many people feel should be left unilluminated. Not that one would suspect it from his appearance. Some men who spend their lives studying abnormalities begin to look distinctly queer themselves, but not Auckland. To look at him one would put him down as a country doctor, a big red-faced man of about sixty, obviously still pretty fit, with a shrewd but kindly face. We belonged to the same club and for years had been on nodding terms, but I didn't discover until quite recently that he was a book-collector, and that only accidentally. I went to refer to Davenport's *Armorial Bookbindings* in the club library, and found him reading it. He deplored its inaccuracies, and I offered to lend him a list of corrections and additions that I had been preparing. This led to further discussion on bindings, and finally he invited me to go back with him to his flat and see his books. It was not yet ten o'clock and I agreed readily.

The night was fine, and we strolled together across the park to Artillery Mansions, where he was living at the time. On arriving we went up in the lift, and were soon seated in the dining-room of his flat, the walls of which were lined with books from floor to ceiling. I was glad to see that one alcove was entirely filled with calf and vellum bindings, the sight of which sent a little thrill of expectation down my spine. I crossed the room to examine them, and my host rose too. A glance showed me that they were all of the class that second-hand booksellers classify comprehensively under the word "Occult". This, however, did not surprise me, as I knew of Auckland's interests. He took down several volumes, and began to expatiate on them—some first editions of the astrological works of Robert Fludd, and a very fine copy of the 1575 *Theatrum Diabolorum*. I expressed my admiration, and we began to talk of trials for witchcraft. He had turned aside to fetch a copy of Scot's *Discoverie* to illustrate some point in his argument when suddenly my eye became riveted on the back of a small book on the top shelf, and my heart missed a beat. Of course it couldn't be, but it was fantastically like it! The same limp vellum cover without any lettering, with the same curious diagonal tear in the vellum at the top of the spine. My hand shook a little as I took it down and opened it. Yes, it was the book. I read once more the title villainously printed on indifferent paper: *Herodes Redivivus seu Liber Scelerosae Vitae et Mortis Sanguinolentae Retzii, Monstri Nannetensis,* Parisiis, MDXLV. As I read the words memories came flooding back of that macabre episode which had overshadowed my school days. Some of the terror that had come to me twenty years before returned, and I felt quite faint.

"I say, you must have a nose for a rarity," said Auckland, pointing to the volume in my hand.

"I've seen this book before," I replied.

"Really?" he said. "I'd be very glad to know where. There's no copy in any public collection in England, and the only one I've traced on the Continent is in the Ambrosian Library at Milan. I haven't even *seen* that. It's in the catalogue, but it's one of those books that librarians are very reluctant to produce. Can you remember where you've met it before?"

"I mean that I've seen this copy before," I answered.

He shook his head dubiously. "I think you must be mistaken about that. I've owned this for nearly twenty years, and before that it was the property of a man that you're most unlikely to have met. In fact, he died in Broadmoor fifteen years ago. His name was—"

"Race," I interposed.

He looked at me with interest. "I shouldn't have expected you to remember that," he said. "You must have been at school during the trial—not that it got much publicity. Thank God, there's legislation to prevent the gutter press from splashing that sort of stuff across their headlines." He half smiled. "You must have been a very precocious child—surely you were only a schoolboy at the time?"

"Yes," I replied. "I was a schoolboy—*the* schoolboy, one might say; the one who gave evidence at the trial and whose name was suppressed."

He put down the book he was holding and looked hard at me. "That's most extraordinarily interesting. I suppose you wouldn't be willing to tell me about it? As you know, cases of that sort are rather my subject. Of course, it would be in the strictest confidence."

I smiled. "There's nothing in my story that I'm particularly ashamed of," I replied, "though I must confess that I occasionally feel that if I'd been a little more intelligent the tragedy might have been averted. However, I've no objection at all. It's only of academic interest now. I haven't thought about the matter for years."

He sat me down in an armchair and poured me out a large whisky-and-soda, then settled himself opposite me.

"Take your time about it," he said. "I'm a very late bird, and it's only a quarter to eleven."

I took a long drink and collected my thoughts.

"I was at a large school on the outskirts of Bristol," I began, "and was not quite sixteen at the time of these events. Even in those days I was extremely interested in old books, a hobby in which I was encouraged by my housemaster. I never cut a great figure on the games field, and when it was wet or I was not put down for a game, I used to go book-hunting in Bristol. Of course, my purse was very limited and my ignorance profound, but I got enormous pleasure out of pottering round the shops and stalls of the town, returning every now and then with a copy of Pope's *Homer* or Theobald's *Shakespeare* to grace my study.

"I don't know whether you're acquainted with Bristol, but it's a most fascinating town. As one descends the hills towards the Avon, one passes from the Georgian crescents and squares of Clifton into the older maritime town, with its magnificent churches and extensive docks. Down by the river are many narrow courts and alleys, which are unchanged since the days when Bristol was a thriving mediaeval port. Much of this poorer area was out of bounds to the boys at school, but having exhausted the bookshops of the University area, I found it convenient to ignore this rule and explored every corner of the old town. One Saturday afternoon—it was in a summer term—I was wandering round the area between St. Mary Redcliffe and the old 'Floating Harbour', and I discovered a little court approached through a narrow passage. It was a miserable enough place, dark and damp, but a joy to the antiquarian—so long as he didn't have to live there! The first floors of the half-timbered houses jutted out and very nearly shut out the sky, and the court ended abruptly in a high blank wall. At the end on the right was a shop—at least the ground-floor window was filled with a collection of books. They were of little interest, and from the accumulation of dust upon them it was obvious that they hadn't been disturbed for years. The place had a deserted air, and it was in no great hope of finding it open that I tried the door. But it did open, and I found myself in its dark interior. Books were everywhere—all the shelves were blocked by great stacks of books on the floor with narrow lanes through which one could barely squeeze sideways, and over everything lay the same thick coating of dust that I'd noticed in the window. I felt as though I were the first person to enter it for years. No bell rang as I opened the door, and I looked round for the proprietor. I saw him sitting in an alcove at my right, and I picked my way through the piles of books to his desk. Did you ever see him yourself?"

"Only later, in Broadmoor," replied Auckland. "I'd like you to describe in your own words exactly how he struck you at the time."

"Well," I resumed, "my first impression of him was the extreme whiteness of his face. One felt on looking at him that he never went out into the sun. He had the unhealthy look that a plant gets if you leave a flower-pot over it and keep the light and air from it. His hair was long and straight and a dirty grey. Another thing that impressed me was the smoothness of his skin. You know how sometimes a man looks as though he has never had any need to shave—attractive in a young man but quite repulsive in an old one—well, that's how he looked. He stood up as I approached, and I saw he was a fat man, not grotesquely so but sufficiently to suggest grossness. His lips particularly were full and fleshy.

"I was half afraid of my own temerity in having entered, but he seemed glad to see me and said in rather a high-pitched voice:

"'Come in, my dear boy; this is a most pleasant surprise. What can I do for you?'

"I mumbled something about being interested in old books and wanting to look round, and he readily assented. Shambling round from pile to pile, he set himself deliberately to interest me. And the man was a fascinating talker—in a very little while he had summed up my small stock of bibliographical knowledge and was enlightening me on dates, editions, issues, values and other points of interest. It was with real regret that I glanced at my watch and found that I had to hurry back to school. I had made no purchase, but he insisted on presenting me with a book, a nicely bound copy of Sterne's *Sentimental Journey*, and made me promise to visit him again as soon as I could."

"Have you still got the Sterne?" asked Auckland.

"No," I said, "my father destroyed it at the time of the trial.

"As the shop was in a part of the town that was strictly out of bounds, I didn't mention my visit to my housemaster, but on the following Thursday it was too wet for cricket and I returned to my newly found friend.

"This time he took me up to a room on the first floor, where there were more books and several portfolios of prints. Race, for such I discovered was his name, was a mine of information on the political history of the eighteenth century, and kept me enthralled by his exposition of a great volume of Gillray cartoons. The man had a sort of magnetism, and at that impressionable age I fell completely under his spell. He drew me out about myself and my work at school, and it was impossible for a boy not to feel flattered by the attention of so learned a man. It was easy to forget his rather repellent physical qualities when he talked so brilliantly.

"Suddenly we heard the shop door below opening, and with an exclamation of annoyance he descended the stairs to attend to the customer. A minute or two passed, and he did not return. I listened and could hear the murmur of conversation below. I idly pulled a book or two from the shelves and glanced at them, but there was little in the room that he had not already shown me. I went to the door and peered down over the stairs, but couldn't see what was going on. My ears caught a scrap of dialogue about the county histories of Somerset. I became bored.

"Across the landing at the top of the stairs was another room, the door of which was very slightly ajar. I'm afraid that I'm of a very inquisitive disposition. I pushed it open and peeped in. It was obviously where Race lived. There was a bed in one corner, a wardrobe, and a circular table in the middle of the room, but what caught my eye at once and held me spellbound was a picture over the fireplace. No words of mine can describe it."

Auckland nodded. "I saw it—an unrecorded Goya—in his most bloodcurdling vein—made his 'Witches' Sabbath' look like a school treat! It was burned by our unimaginative police force. They wouldn't even let me photograph it." He sighed.

I resumed. "I went nearer to have a look at it. On the mantelpiece below it was a book—the book you've got now on your top shelf. I opened it and read the title page. Of course it meant nothing to me. Gille de Retz doesn't feature in the average school curriculum. Suddenly I heard a noise behind me and swung round. There was Race standing in the doorway. He had come up the stairs without my hearing him. I shall never forget the blazing fury in his eyes. His face seemed whiter than ever as he stood there, a terrifying figure literally shaking with rage.

"I quickly tried to make my apologies, but he silenced me with a gesture; then he snatched the book from my hands and replaced it on the mantelpiece. Still without speaking, he pointed to the door and I went quickly down the stairs. He followed me down into the shop. I was about to leave without another word when suddenly his whole manner changed. It was as though he had recollected some powerful reason for conciliating me. He laid a hand on my arm.

"'My dear boy,' he said, 'you must forgive my momentary annoyance. I am a methodical man, and I can't bear people touching the things in my room. I'm afraid that living as something of a recluse has made me rather fussy. I quite realise that you meant no harm. There are some very valuable books and pictures in there—not for sale, but my own private collection, and naturally I can't allow customers to wander in and out of it in my absence.'

"I expressed my contrition awkwardly enough, for the whole situation had embarrassed me horribly and I felt ill at ease. He perceived this and added:

"'Now you mustn't worry about this—and least of all must you let it stop you coming here. I want you to promise that you'll visit me as soon as you can again—just to show that you bear no ill-will. I'll hunt out some interesting things for you to look at.'

"I gave him my promise and hurried back to school. In a day or two I had persuaded myself that I'd been imagining things, that some trick of the light had made him appear so distorted with rage. After all, why should a man get so angry about so little? As for the picture, it made comparatively little impression on my schoolboy mind. Much that it depicted was unintelligible to me at that time. I was, in any case, unlikely to be invited into the private room again. And so I resolved to pay a further visit to the shop.

"An opportunity didn't occur for nearly a fortnight, and when I did manage to slip down to Bristol, there was no mistaking how glad he was to see me. He was almost gushing in his manner. He had been as good as his word in finding more books to show me, and I spent a most pleasant afternoon. Race was as voluble as ever, but I got the impression that he was slightly distrait, as though he were labouring under some sort of suppressed excitement. Several times as I looked up from a book I caught him looking at me in a queer reflective way, which made me feel a little uncomfortable. When I finally said that I must go, he made a suggestion that he had never made before.

"'You've got very dusty,' he said. 'You really must wash your hands before you go. There's a basin downstairs—I'll turn on the light for you.'

"As he said this, he stepped across the shop, opened a door and turned a switch, illuminating a long flight of stairs. I descended them. They were of stone and led apparently into a cellar. As I reached the bottom step the light was extinguished. I turned sharply and saw him standing at the head of the stairs—a fantastic, foreshortened figure at the top of the shaft, silhouetted in the doorway. He had his hands stretched out, holding on to the jambs of the door, and with the half-light of the shop behind him he looked like a misshapen travesty of a cross. I called out to him and started to remount the stairs, but as I did so he quickly closed the door without saying a word.

"I was terribly afraid. Of course, it might have been a joke but I knew inside me that it wasn't and that I was in the most deadly peril. I reached the top of the stairs and groped at the door, but there seemed to be no handle inside. I couldn't find the switch either, it must have been in the shop. I shouted, there was no reply. An awful horror gripped me—the dank smell of the stone cellar, the lack of air and the darkness, all conspired to undermine what little courage I possessed. I shouted again; then listened, holding my breath. All at once I heard the outer shop door open and an unfamiliar footstep inside the shop. With all my strength I pounded on the door, shouting and screaming like a madman. The noise reverberating

round the confined space nearly deafened me. I listened again for
a second; voices were raised in the shop, but I caught no words. I
shouted again until I felt my lungs would burst and hammered on
the door until my fists were bruised. Suddenly it was flung open and
I stumbled out, hysterical with fear and half-blinded by the daylight.
Before me stood an old clergyman, behind him Race, who bore on
his face the same look of malevolent fury that I had seen before.

"'What is the matter?' asked the clergyman. 'How did you get
shut in there?'

"It was then that I made my fatal mistake. All I wanted was
to get away and never come back again. If I lodged a complaint
I foresaw endless trouble, with the school authorities, even with
the police. My terror had evaporated with the daylight, and I was
feeling more than a little ashamed of myself.

"'I went down to wash my hands,' I said. 'The lights went out
and I got frightened. I'm quite all right now, though.'

"The clergyman looked enquiringly at Race, but the latter had
recovered his self-possession.

"'The lights must have fused,' he said; 'they often do—it's the
damp. I was just going to let him out when you came in. No wonder
he was frightened. It's a most eerie place in the dark.'

"The clergyman looked from him to me, as if inviting some
comment from me, but I merely said, 'I ought to be getting back
to school now.'

"We left the shop together, and as we walked through the passage out of the court I looked back, and there was Race standing on
the step of his shop following us with baleful eyes. My companion
seemed to be debating whether he would ask me a question, but he
refrained. I hardly liked to ask him to say nothing about the episode;
he obviously wished to satisfy his curiosity, but we were complete

strangers and, though old enough to be my grandfather, he seemed to be a diffident man. It was a curious relationship.

"He put me on to a bus, and I thanked him gravely. As we shook hands he said abruptly, 'I shouldn't go there again,' and turned away.

"For a few days I was on tenterhooks lest he should make any report of the occurrence to the school, but as the days became weeks and I heard no more, my mind became at rest. I had firmly decided that nothing would induce me to visit Race's shop again, and soon the whole episode assumed an air of unreality in my mind."

I looked at my watch.

"Good Lord!" I said to Auckland, "it's getting pretty late. Do you want to go to bed? We could have another session tomorrow."

"Certainly not," he replied. "I find your story of the most absorbing interest. It fills in all sorts of gaps in my knowledge of the affair. If you don't mind sitting up, I should greatly appreciate it if you'd carry on."

He refilled my glass and I settled myself more comfortably into my chair.

"Well," I continued, "I'm a bit diffident about telling the rest of the story. Up to now it's been pretty strange, but it has been sober fact; now we get into realms where I find myself a bit out of my depth."

Auckland nodded. "Never mind," he said, "let's have it. Just as it comes back to you—don't try to explain it, just tell me what happened."

"A year passed and I was still at school," I continued; "I'd got into the Sixth Form and was working pretty hard for a scholarship. I'd also got into the House Cricket XI by some miracle, and so I couldn't be so free and easy about games as I had been previously.

Public opinion forced me to take them fairly seriously. A dropped catch at a critical point in a match can make a schoolboy's life pretty good hell.

"At that age I used to sleep extraordinarily well—I still do for that matter. It was very rare for me to dream and then only of trivial affairs. But on the night of June 26th—I noted the date in my diary—I had the first of a couple of particularly horrible dreams. I dreamed most vividly that I was back in Race's shop. Every detail of that untidy interior passed in an accurate picture through my brain. I was standing in the middle of the shop, and it was dusk. Very little light came through those dusty windows piled high with books. Race himself was nowhere to be seen. The door to the cellar which had such sinister associations for me was closed. Suddenly from the other side of it came a series of appalling screams and shouts, intermingled with muffled bangs and thumps on the door. I ran across and tried to open it, but it was locked. Then I darted out to the shop steps to see if anyone were at hand to assist me, but the court was deserted. I stood irresolute in the shop, and then all at once the cries seemed to get weaker and the banging on the door ceased. I listened and could hear the sounds of a struggle on the stairs gradually getting fainter as it reached the cellar below.

"At this point I awoke shivering with fright, bathed in a cold sweat. Sleep was impossible for me during the rest of the night. I lay and thought about my dream. It seemed so queer that I should dream, not of my own experience on the stairs, but from the point of view of an observer.

"The next night exactly the same thing occurred, and the horror of the scene so impressed me that I must have cried out in my sleep, for I found that I'd awakened several of the other boys in my dormitory. I couldn't bear the anticipation of having such a dream a third time, and I went to the House Matron on the following day and told her that I couldn't sleep. She moved me from the dormitory into the sick-room and gave me a sedative. On that night and thereafter I slept quite normally again.

"Not quite a fortnight later a further link was forged in this extraordinary chain of events. I was passing the local police-station and I stopped to read a notice posted outside about the protection of wild birds—I've always been a bit of an ornithologist. Along the railings in front of the building were hung the usual medley of notices—Lost, Found and Missing. My eye caught one more recent than the others—and I idly read it.

"I cannot, of course, remember the exact wording at this date, but it asked for information about a boy named Roger Weyland, aged fifteen and a half. He was described in detail, and I remember being struck at once by his similarity to myself. He had left his home at Clevedon after lunch on June 26th to bicycle into Bristol, where he intended to visit the docks. He was last seen near St. Mary Redcliffe at about half-past five the same afternoon, and the police were asking anyone to come forward who could throw light on his whereabouts.

"I read and reread the notice. Its implication dawned on me at once. It's no good asking why, but I assure you that at the moment I *knew* what had happened. My dream of the night of June 26th was still fresh in my memory, and even in the broad sunlit street I shuddered and was oppressed by a feeling of nameless horror.

"I debated what I should do. The police, I felt sure, would laugh at me. I could never bring myself to walk into the station and blurt out such a fantastic tale to some grinning sergeant. But I must tell someone; and after dinner that day I sought an interview with my housemaster. He was a most understanding man, and listened in patient silence while I told him the whole story. I must have spoken with conviction, because at the end of it he rang up a friend of his, a local Inspector of Police. Half an hour later I repeated my tale to him. He was very polite, asked one or two searching questions, but I could see that he was sceptical. He did, however, agree with my housemaster that Race's activities might profitably be looked into.

"If you followed the trial, I suppose you know all the rest—how they found the boy's body and God-knows-what other devilish things beside. My name was suppressed in the evidence, and I left school at the end of that term and went abroad for six months.

"One very odd thing about it all was that they never traced the clergyman. The police were most anxious to get him to corroborate my story, and my father was equally keen to find him—after all, he saved my life—and my father wanted to show some tangible appreciation of the fact, subscribe generously to one of his favourite charities or something. It's very queer really that the police, with all their nation-wide organisation, never got on to him. After all, there aren't a limitless number of clergymen, and the number of those in the Bristol area that afternoon must have been comparatively small. Perhaps he didn't like to come forward and be connected with such a business, but I don't think that's very likely—he didn't strike me as the sort of man who would shirk his obligations.

"That's really all that I can tell you, and I expect you knew some of that already."

"A certain amount," replied Auckland, "but by no means all. I occasionally get asked questions by the police in this kind of case, and I did assist them on this occasion, though I wasn't called in evidence. Race had a damned good counsel in Rutherford, and

managed to convince the jury that he was insane. If a man is sufficiently wicked, a British jury will often believe that he must be
mad. And so he went to Broadmoor. Of course, he was as sane as
you and I are."

"How did you come to get hold of one of his books?" I asked.

"Through the good offices of the police," he said. "Perhaps as
a sort of consolation prize for my distress at the destruction of the
Goya. The book is really the clue to Race.

"It is a contemporary account of the activities of Gille de Retz,
Marshal of France, hanged at Nantes in 1440. I expect you know a
certain amount about him; he figures in all the standard works on
Diabolism. The contemporary authorities are a bit vague on the
exact number of children he murdered—Monstrelet says a hundred
and sixty, but Chastellain and some others put it at a hundred and
forty. But all this is general knowledge.

"What isn't so widely known is that every now and then he
seems to reappear in history—at least the devilish practices, with
which his name is associated, crop up again and again. He was
quite a cult in seventeenth-century Venice, and there was a case in
Bohemia in the middle of the last century. A variant of de Retz's
name is de Rais and Race himself claimed to be a descendant; but
I've no proof of this. The police failed to trace his parentage or to
find any details about him before he appeared in Bristol just before
the First World War. His shop has gone now; the whole of that area
was pulled down in a recent slum-clearance scheme.

"The trial at Nantes in 1440 has always been an interest of
mine, and I had a great find the last time I was in Paris. Some early
Nantes archives had recently been acquired by the Bibliothèque
Nationale, and I spent a happy week examining all the original
documents relating to the examination of the woman, La Meffrie,

who procured most of the children for de Retz. I've got transcripts of the most important. Would you care to borrow them? They are quite enthralling."

"Not on your life," I replied as I rose to take my leave. "I came far too near to playing the principal role to read about such things with any pleasure. *You* may be able to take a detached, scientific view of the case, but, believe me, I've had enough of de Retz and all his works to last me a lifetime."

THE WORK OF EVIL (1963)

William Croft Dickinson (1897–1963)

William Croft Dickinson was a distinguished historian. In 1943 he became the first ever English-born person to be appointed to the Sir William Fraser Professorship of Scottish History and Palaeography, a prestigious Chair at the University of Edinburgh. It was whilst working there that he began writing ghost stories, the first of which ('The Sweet Singers') was published in *Blackwood's Magazine* in February 1947.

'The Work of Evil' was published in Dickinson's short-story collection *Dark Encounters* (1963). In it, librarians discover an uncatalogued *incunabulum*—a Latin word meaning "from the cradle" and referring to a book printed in the fifteenth century, at the very beginning of Western printing. It is a potent story with which to end this volume, and a warning to librarians everywhere who try to make their collections more accessible.

E VER SINCE HIS RETURN TO DUTY FROM HIS LONG ILLNESS,
Maitland Allan, our Keeper of Printed Books, had been singularly reluctant to grant any access to the Special Collections which
were in his charge; so much so that the Rare Book Room in the
library had become well-nigh as sacred and as difficult to enter as
the secret courts of an Eastern harem. Thus, when he suddenly
said to me: "Come, and I'll show you the whole collection," I was
taken completely by surprise.

I had asked for an early Italian work by Aeneas Sylvius. The
assistant at the library counter had disappeared with my form.
Allan had come back with him. And now, strangely, I was to be
shown "the whole collection". Was this simply a piece of unexpected good fortune? Or had the old man some ulterior purpose?
I had noticed during the last two or three weeks that he had made
a point of stopping to talk to me whenever we met in a room or
corridor. Had he singled me out in some way from the rest of my
colleagues? And if so, why? Everyone knew that his recent illness
had made him a little "queer".

Opening a door marked "Staff Only", Allan led the way through
a maze of book-lined passages until at last, passing a heavy steel
door, we stopped before an inner iron grille. This he unlocked and,
stepping aside, he ushered me into the room.

I glanced around with curiosity; but he gave me time for no
more than a quick glance.

"There they are," he said, pointing to one of the stacks. 'An
extraordinary collection. A frightening collection. The *Lucretia and*

Eurialus which you want happens to be in it, but it's very much of a stranger there. For the rest, I hate them,' and his voice rose nervously as if in emphasis.

I walked over to the stack, but I noticed he did not accompany me. There, as I saw two long rows of beautiful bindings, I murmured something of my appreciation and delight. Reverently taking down one volume after another, I examined the bindings more closely. All were of rich leather elaborately tooled in a variety of intricate patterns in which whorls and strange cabalistic signs predominated. I also turned to the title-pages: every work was either an *incumabulum* or of a date early in the sixteenth century. But every work was on the same theme. I ran my eye along the shelves, picking out the volumes which bore titles on their spines. Still the same theme.

"Why!" I exclaimed, turning towards him; "they are all on black magic and necromancy. What you might call a collection of evil; or at any rate a collection of evil intent. Who on earth gathered together all this devilry? It looks as though someone was striving hard to find something which at last would work."

"An unfortunate young man whose history you know as well as I do," answered Allan, slowly. "John, third Earl of Gowrie. You may remember that after studying here he became a law student at Padua, and was there said to have dabbled in magic and witchcraft. Well, here's his library—or part of it. And I wish it had never survived."

Again I noticed the nervous pitch in his voice.

"Well," I replied, lightly, "if he did dabble in the forbidden art he must have found it pretty ineffective. The very number of his books shows that. One would have thought that constant experiment followed by constant failure and disappointment would have been bound to bring disillusion."

For a full minute Allan made no reply. Instead, he gazed at me with an odd look in his eyes.

"'Ineffective'!" he said, at last. "I wish to God you were right! Do you see that safe over there? It contains one further book belonging to Gowrie's collection. No one knows it is there but myself—and now you. That book is the one book which, at last, Gowrie found *would* work. Listen to me—you *must* listen to me—and I'll tell you a tale of devilry that has tormented me ever since this collection came in. Then you'll believe in 'effectiveness'."

He had pointed to a small safe in a corner of the room. I made a step towards it, but he seized me by the arm.

"Often I feel I must take the book in that safe and throw it into the middle of the sea," he continued, "but I can't do it. I'm too afraid. Only one small book, yet it is evil itself. That one book seizes a man by the throat and strangles him to death."

I looked at him in astonishment. Could it be Allan who was saying all this, and who was holding my arm so tightly that his fingers were biting into my flesh?

"Whatever do you mean?" I asked, partly disturbed, and partly angry at being held as though I were a child faced with something which might be dangerous.

"I wish I knew," he replied slowly, and in a quieter tone. "All I can tell you is that within the last eighteen months two men have been strangled to death after looking into that book. That's all."

I was dumbstruck. And not without reason. We stood there, tense and silent, like two conspirators surprised by something they couldn't name and fearful of what it might mean.

The collection came to us towards the end of the war, said Allan, breaking the silence at last. It came from the local Antiquarian

Society, and it came in the wooden boxes in which it had been stored when Gowrie House was pulled down in 1805 and in which it had remained, untouched, until we opened those boxes in this very room nearly one hundred and fifty years later. It is said that the books were discovered in a wall closet which had been panelled in and so lost to sight. It may well be so. Perhaps Gowrie himself entombed them that way. Perhaps he, too, tried to rid himself of an evil incubus. Perhaps Gowrie put one particular book, with all its fellows, into a hidden closet, as I have put that one particular book into a safe. Perhaps he, too, was afraid to do the one thing he ought to have done. Or perhaps he did something else. Perhaps he put his own curse upon the book that no one should again open its pages and live. That, at any rate, has been its history here.

First it was Fraser, who, you will remember, was our professor of chemistry before you came. As soon as the collection arrived he was all agog to see it. Day after day he was here with his note-book. "Working out their formulae," he would say to me. "Damned interesting, some of them."

But one day he read too much. I had been in the Reid Room that afternoon, and I didn't come here until nearly closing time. Fraser, as usual, was in his seat by the window there; but, that afternoon, he didn't look up with his usual cheery nod. Instead, as he looked up at my entrance, I saw that his face was drawn and white. "My God, Allan," he said in a strained voice, "this book is the Devil himself. It should be burned. Burned to ashes." He pushed his chair back and seemed to recover himself. "Look," he continued, glaring at me with fierce earnestness, "I'm putting it here, in this empty case. Lock it in. And let no one, no one, ever read it again."

He strode to that wire-fronted case over there—it was empty then—thrust in the book, and waited for me to lock the door with my master key. Then he pushed past me and went out. It was the last I saw of him.

That same night he was found dead in his own room in the lab. Strangled. And no one could explain how or why.

He had a queer kind of lab-coat of which he was very proud. It was like an old-fashioned smock which was tied by a fancy cord running through the neck. When he was found, his hands were gripping that cord. It had been drawn so tight that it had throttled him. The students working in the lab had seen no one go into his room or come out of it. I know now that they *wouldn't* see anyone. I know, too, that Fraser's hands were at that cord in a vain struggle to loosen it, and live.

No one thought of connecting Fraser's death with the book he had been reading. At first I hardly associated the two events myself. Yet it was not long before I found I was growing frightened of that book, lying by itself in its locked case. I tried to avoid looking at it, but it seemed to force its presence upon me. Perhaps a fortnight passed before I realised the truth. Then, suddenly, I knew. I knew that Fraser's death had been caused by it.

Frightened as I was, I still had courage enough to do one thing. Unknown to the rest of the staff, I removed from the library catalogue all the entries relating to it. Fraser's death should not go unheeded. No one should read that book again. No one should even know of its existence. Had I dared, I would have burned it—as Fraser had said it should be burned. But I couldn't bring myself to touch it. Already it had me in its power. I was afraid of it. And so young Inglis had to die. A second victim.

He had come to us as a part-time student assistant, and had quickly proved his worth. So much so that special tasks were soon assigned to him automatically. And, at a time when I was unluckily

absent for a few days with influenza, he was given the task of checking the shelf catalogue of the Special Collections. You can imagine
my horror when, on the day of my return to duty, I found him here,
holding *the book* in his hands, open, and reading it.

As soon as he saw me he called out: "I've found an *incunabulum*
which is not in the catalogue. It's filthy with dust…"

But I rushed up and seized the thing from him. I shoved it
back into the case and relocked the door, while he looked at me
open-mouthed. But what could I say? I simply dare not tell him
the truth. As I saw it, to tell him the truth would be to tell him his
own sentence of death. I made some feeble excuse, which I know
he didn't believe, and sent him off. Then I sat down, sick and faint.
What could I do to save him? Nothing. He was doomed. The evil
thing was upon him, and he could never escape. I cursed myself for
my own cowardice. Why, at least, had I not warned him? Had the
book so laid its spell upon me that I even feared the ridicule which
might follow my warning?

Poor beggar. He didn't escape. When the library was closing
that night, one of the staff found that the automatic lift wouldn't
work. Naturally he assumed that someone, on one of the floors, had
failed to shut the door properly; and he went to look. He found the
door which wasn't shut. He also found Inglis. He was trapped by the
outer door, and, strangely, he was trapped by the neck. Almost as
though he had entered the lift and then, as the door was sliding-to,
had put out his head to look at something. Stranger still, but only
to those who didn't know what I knew, the poor fellow was dead.
I tell you, the pressure of the outer doors on that lift is so light that
you can hold them back easily with one hand. Yet Inglis was dead.
He had been throttled by the light pressure of a lift-door. Fraser had
been strangled on the day he had opened the book. So had Inglis.

Can you wonder that the same night I had what was called a nervous break-down?

I was away for over a year and, as you probably know, I have only been back for some six weeks or so. Surprisingly, I have kept my reason—though sometimes I'm not sure. Perhaps I am mad; or perhaps I am suffering from some delusion. Yet I was the only person who knew that Inglis had opened the book; I was the only person who knew that Inglis was doomed to die. And he did die. As Fraser had died.

God forgive me! I should destroy the thing. But I daren't. I am too afraid of it. Yet about a fortnight ago, the day I spoke to you in the Upper Hall, I was brave enough to move it out of the book-case and to lock it away in that safe. You gave me the courage to do that—even though you didn't know you had done so. Now, I am afraid again. I feel it is laughing at me behind that steel door... and biding its time.

You *must* forgive me; but I *had* to tell you all this. One day I, too, may be found strangled. And you, at least, will know the reason why.

As you may imagine, I was not particularly pleased at having this extraordinary burden of knowledge so suddenly thrust upon me. Yet, as I crossed the Quad back to my own room, my thoughts ran in a different vein. "Poor old Allan," I thought. "No wonder he had a breakdown. No wonder he is 'queer'. Fancy living with *that* on your mind all the time. Poor wretch! A victim to his own imagination: with a harmless book locked up in his safe, and fearing it as though it possessed all the malignant power of some genie in the *Arabian Nights*. And mortally afraid to do the one thing which would bring relief."

But I did Allan an injustice.

I had given my lecture next morning, and was talking to a student in my retiring-room, when Wallace, one of the lecturers in the Modern Languages Department, and Allan's next-door neighbour, opened the door and beckoned me outside.

"Did you know Maitland Allan was dead?" he asked.

"Dead?" I repeated.

"Yes. Apparently last night he was all worked up about something. Kept walking up and down his study, saying in a loud voice: 'I *will* do it. I *will* do it'; and generally worrying his housekeeper out of her wits. Then, suddenly, about nine o'clock, she heard him go into the hall. Peeping round her door she saw him put on a cap, his scarf and his overcoat, and literally rush out of the house.

"By this time thoroughly alarmed, she came to us. I did my best to calm her down, but she was so upset that in the end I offered to go back with her and to wait up with her for Allan's return.

"He didn't come in until nearly two o'clock in the morning. We heard him open the front door and then, just when he had shut it again, we heard him give a queer kind of strangled, choking cry. We rushed into the hall and saw him half-hanging from the door and half-sprawled on the rug in the hall. One end of his scarf had caught in the door as he had shut it and, when he had turned away, it had pulled tight round his neck and had trapped him. We opened the door at once and released him, but, when we tried to help him to his feet again, we discovered to our horror that he was dead... I came over to tell you for I believe he had taken quite a liking to you..."

But I was no longer listening. My thoughts were rushing madly towards one word which seemed to loom larger and larger. And the one word was "strangled". Fraser; Inglis; Allan. Could it *all* be coincidence? Or could such things indeed be true?

*

Naturally the Procurator Fiscal conducted an inquiry into Allan's death.

A boatman stated that Allan (whom he identified) had knocked him up about midnight and had asked to be rowed "a full mile out to sea". At first he had demurred, for Allan had seemed "fair demented"; but an offer of five pounds had seemingly settled the matter. He had rowed Allan out to sea and, when he had told him that they were well beyond the full mile for which he had asked, Allan, to his utter surprise, had suddenly plucked a small book from his coat pocket, had raised it with both hands above his head, and had hurled it down into the water with all his force. Then, said the boatman, "he crouched him down in the boat as though he were afraid someone was going to hit him. And he stayed like that till I tied up again, when he jumped out of the boat and fair ran along the quay as if the Devil himself was chasing him."

The doctors were puzzled, but unanimous. Despite the softness and natural elasticity of the scarf, they had been surprised to find a sharp mark around Allan's neck. But they were convinced he had died of shock. His heart, they said, was in poor condition; any shock would probably be too much for it.

And I alone knew what that "shock" would be. I alone knew what would flash through the poor wretch's mind when he felt that sudden, unexpected tightening of his scarf around his neck.

So much I had written yesterday when my mind was free. But how different is today! Today all Allan's fear and dread are now my own. Today, at the close of the Library Committee, our librarian spoke casually, as of a matter of little importance. He had looked over the Rare Book Room, he said, after Allan's death, and there he had found, inside the safe, a book that belonged to the Gowrie Collection but which, to his surprise, *had no entry in the catalogue.*

Dazed and bewildered, I have found my way back to my room. And, as I write this down, I am a prey to every wild imagining. Can it be that Allan, deranged and overwrought on that last fearful night, cast the wrong book away? How could he? It was the only book within the safe. Yet reason recoils from that other thought—that a book can return from the depths of the sea. Reason? How long can reason prevail against this fearful question that is now pulsing through my mind? Already our librarian has handled the book, and opened it.

Also Available

LOST IN A PYRAMID

And Other Classic Mummy Stories

A mummy disappears from its sarcophagus in the dead of night; a crazed Egyptologist entombs a beautiful young woman; a student at Oxford reveals the terrible secrets of an ancient papyrus.

These are among the twelve tales from the golden age of the mummy story collected here – stories that still cast a spell with their different versions of the mummy's curse, some chilling, others darkly romantic and even comic.

Including tales by major writers such as Arthur Conan Doyle and Louisa May Alcott, as well as rare discoveries unearthed for the first time in over 100 years, this enthralling collection is introduced by Andrew Smith, a leading expert on ghost stories and Victorian Gothic.

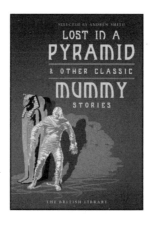

PAPERBACK £8.99   ISBN 978 0 7123 5617 6